Geoff coul~~~~~~~ ~ ~~~~ t
when npo
dates for 2

G000241381

npower Ashes
Test Series 2009

Cardiff Wed 8 - Sun 12 July
Lord's Thurs 16 - Mon 20 July
Edgbaston Thurs 30 July - Mon 3 Aug
Headingley Carnegie Fri 7 - Tues 11 Aug
Brit Oval Thurs 20 - Mon 24 Aug

i

We at Corporate Occasions pride ourselves on having the biggest balls in Birmingham, or anywhere else, for that matter.

We specialize in high-quality catering, summer balls, marquee hire, conference production, entertainment - you name it, we can handle it; from a small, intimate event to a sit-down dinner for a thousand people, with ice sculptures, live music, celebrity guests and a fly-past by the Red Arrows. Occasionally, we even let Geoff Tristram draw caricatures around the tables for us, when he's not too busy writing his silly books, and *very* occasionally we actually pay him!

Don't get caught out when you're organizing your next event. After all, why settle for a four, when you could have a six? Give Corporate Occasions a ring, and let us handle *your* balls!

Geoff Tristram has been a professional artist and cartoonist for over twenty-five years, working for a diverse range of clients including Penguin, Embassy World Snooker, The BBC, Tarmac, Carillion, Past Times, Winsor & Newton, Trivial Pursuit and the television show, 'They Think It's All Over!', to name but a few.

He has created artwork featuring celebrities such as Jonathan Ross, Jeremy Clarkson, Ian Botham, David Vine, Alan Shearer, Ian Hislop and Gary Lineker, not to mention virtually every famous snooker player that ever lifted a cue. You may have even noticed him at the World Championships on TV, interviewing them as he drew their caricatures!

He has also designed many book covers, album sleeves for bands such as UB40, The Maisonettes and City Boy, (remember them?) and postage stamps, notably 'Charles and Diana - The Royal Wedding', 'Miss World', 'Lake Placid Winter Olympics' and 'Spain 1982 World Cup Football' editions.

More recently, his series of incredibly detailed 'Cat Conundrum' puzzle paintings have enthralled and exasperated thousands of dedicated puzzle-solvers all over the world.

Geoff's younger brother, David, is a well-known and extremely successful comedy playwright, so it was no real surprise when Geoff eventually turned his hand to comedy writing, hence this, his sixth full-length novel, featuring the chaotic and accident-prone artist, David Day.

In order to make up for lost time, Geoff has now written a total of seven novels following this dreamy, scatterbrained character as he grows up and eventually gets a real job. Geoff's family wonders if he will do likewise.

Stealing the Ashes

Geoff Tristram

Having given up all hope
of you actually buying one,
I have been reduced to the
sorry state of foisting one
on you for a Christmas present.

**DRAWING
ROOM**

Merry Tristmas,
you tight-arsed bastards.
love Geoff x

First published in 2008 by Geoff Tristram Ltd.

Printed and bound by CPI Antony Rowe, Eastbourne.

ISBN 978-0-9551428-5-7

Cover illustration by Geoff Tristram.

Contact the author on gt@geofftristram.co.uk

With grateful thanks to Aileen Fraser for editing my books. She's a Scottish lady who now lives in France. No wonder her English is dodgy!

carillion

Dear Mr Tristram

Having forked out hundreds of pounds to sponsor your previous books, I am sorry to say we can no longer stretch to the sponsorship of a further publication, no matter how topical it may be.

This decision has not been taken lightly. I have had serious discussions with our Sales Prevention Officer, Ivor Bowness and it appears that not a single enquiry for a new motorway or hospital has been received from advertisements placed in your publications.

We have even approached your colleagues at Enville Cricket Club, who have blatantly refused our offer to redevelop the ground into luxury apartments, with marina.

Although we always try to sponsor local talent (even writers) the current economic climate precludes further commitment. All I can do is enclose a couple of corporate umbrellas for you to auction at the club - please return 50% of any funds raised to me to offset the cost of previous advertisements.

Regards

John Thorpe
Group Brand Manager (Retired)

This is the seventh and final book about David Day (I've also written a prequel to 'A Nasty Bump on the Head' which will be out soon). Mind you, I did say more-or-less the same thing after the previous one, and I meant it at the time, but then I had this great idea pop into my head, and – well, you know what I'm like.

This time it's a story set in and around a cricket club, but don't let that put you off. You don't need to know anything about the game whatsoever to understand this book, and it doesn't matter if you're not familiar with David Day books either. I must warn you though, that both are equally addictive, as I have discovered to my peril. It's only a matter of time before you're caught, book in hand, laughing like a deranged fool on the train as you speed home to catch the test highlights.

Enville Cricket Club, where this story is set, really exists, though the characters are entirely fictional. (Believe that and you'll believe anything.) The club is situated in the beautiful grounds of Enville Hall, a South Staffordshire stately home, which in Victorian times was considered one of the best, largest, flattest and prettiest grounds in the world. My lad, Jamie, plays for the youth team, the seconds, the thirds, the midweek league, the Sunday league and anyone else who'll have him. He's been going there every weekend for four years – at least, I hope he has. Either that or he's got a woman. Highly unlikely as he's still only fourteen, I admit, but the way the world is nowadays, you never know.

When I dropped him off there for his first training session, I instantly fell in love with the place. It seemed to speak to the very depths of my soul. W.G. Grace once played at Enville for an England side, and notched up a rather mediocre ten runs in the first innings and fourteen in the second. I believe he was dismissed 'Beard Before Wicket'.

Like most village clubs, fundraising is a perennial problem. One year they need a new pavilion, the next, new nets and a bowling machine. Personally, I can think of worse ways to spend my money than trying to preserve our cricket pitches. That's why I'm rather foolishly agreeing to donate a portion of the profits (if any) from this very book to Enville C.C. And while we're talking money, I would like to use this opportunity to thank my wonderful sponsors yet again for helping to finance this undoubted masterpiece, and also for their generous donations to the Enville coffers.

On the cricket fields of England our children learn how to play the greatest game on earth, but even more importantly, they also learn about good manners, leadership, teamwork, courage, concentration and fair play. Where else but on a cricket pitch could you hear a team captain asking his players to applaud the winning team, or call for three cheers?

I know it sounds like a corny scene from a circa 1958 Jennings book, but I can assure you that it happens today, and not just at the posh private schools either.

The cricket club has given my boy a purpose, and saved him from spending his weekends hanging around in bus-stops, spitting, smoking and scrawling graffiti.

He has to do that on Mondays now.

Geoff Tristram

"All that glisters is not gold"

William Shakespeare

Chapter 1

Chewing the Fat

"Don't take this personally," said Laz, draining the remainder of his pint, "but you're getting a right bloody gut on you."

David weighed this as he finished off his sausage roll.

"Why is it that every time someone begins a conversation with, 'Don't take this personally,' they inevitably follow it up with an incredibly personal comment?"

David's observation was momentarily interrupted by a particularly fine cover-drive from Enville's opening batsman. Polite applause concluded, David returned to his theme.

"And besides, isn't what you just said a blatant case of the saucepan calling the teapot black, or whatever the expression is? I am known for my thinness. My waist is just over thirty-two, and at the age of almost forty, I'd consider that a minor triumph, whereas you probably wear a size that's well off the flipping Richter scale, if trousers are governed by Richter scales. You've got a bloody cheek telling me I'm fat. I'm just over twelve stone, and I bet you're at least sixteen."

"Ah! But I'm *supposed* to be a bit big," countered Laz, "whereas, you have always had a reputation for being thin, as you say. The thing about reputations, though, is that you have to earn them by retaining the status quo, and currently, old pal, you aren't, because you've put on a bit of weight, and all I did was to gently remind you of the fact. I don't know why you felt the need to attack me in such a personal way. I was doing you a favour. I'm past caring about myself, but you're still redeemable."

The Enville batsman who had earlier thrilled the meagre crowd with his cover drive now disappointed them with his failure to deal with Himley's leg-spinner. Dismissed and disgruntled, the batsman kicked the two remaining wickets up in the air and slumped back to the pavilion, throwing his bat at a strutting magpie en-route, in retaliation for some perceived slight.

"And I don't buy that '*just over* thirty-two inch waist' stuff either," Laz continued, once the drama was over, "or that crap about being '*just over* twelve stone'. I could say I was *just over* twelve stone as well. Four stone over, to be precise."

"If you must know," replied David haughtily, "My waist is precisely thirty-three, but I have to buy thirty-four trousers and wear a belt, because you can't often get thirty-three trousers, and, for your information, I'm about an ounce over twelve stone, not the weight of a well-fed seven-year-old child over, like you."

It was Laz's turn to be indignant. "Yes, well it suits me, a bit of weight. It makes me look healthier, my mother says. You look like a Buxted oven-ready chicken in your swimming trunks. You're a thin chap with a fat stomach, the worst possible combination, whereas I'm more your noble, Henry the Eighth-type figure - large, but properly proportioned."

David was on the ropes, and still reeling from Laz's cruel comment about the chicken. His friend, smelling victory, tried to land the killer blow.

"And the last time I saw legs like that...."

"What? They were hanging out of a nest?" queried David, incredulously. "Jeez, Laz, the old ones are the best ones aren't they?"

2

Now Laz was staggering. If there was anything that could penetrate his armour, it was an accusation that he had regurgitated old and hackneyed comedy material. Laz was proud of his repertoire, and kept it fresh, if a tad blue on occasion.

"Do you honestly think I would resort to such Christmas cracker stuff?" he asked his oldest friend, with a pained look.

"So what *were* you going to say?" asked David, eyeing him with suspicion.

"Eh? Oh....well played, J.B! What a cracking boundary! Did you see that?" roared Laz, standing up and clapping just a little too enthusiastically.

"Anyway, your mother might think you look healthier," David gamely continued, knowing full-well his friend had tried to change the subject, "but being overweight isn't good, and smoking doesn't help either. At least I'm a non-smoker. You were right though, I have got a bit of a spare tyre. It could be worse — I could have had a spare-tyre factory like you've got — but it's about time I did something about it nevertheless. That's the trouble with having a sedentary job. We artists just sit at drawing boards all day, getting round shoulders and fat stomachs."

"So do we pub and restaurant refurbishers."

"Exactly! We need to make a New Year's Resolution, I think."

"It's the middle of May. Don't think me pedantic. I merely point it out."

"Okay," sighed David theatrically, "a Middle-of-the-Year Resolution. We both need to begin a regime."

Laz stared at him with blank incredulity. "Why?"

"Because, my fat, unfit friend, forty is the time when those who have let themselves go are prone to keeling over with heart attacks, strokes, and the like. You are probably just a walking blubbery mountain of cholesterol with tar-filled lungs nowadays. I doubt if you'll see fifty. My own problems are less serious, but I need to shake this newly-acquired Oven Ready Chicken tag before it comes home to roost. We, my morbidly obese, lardy-arsed old companion, need to get fit, as of now."

Laz had a look of genuine horror on his face. He reached for his half-eaten pork pie, by way of comfort.

"You *are* kidding. A spell in the gym would finish me."

"And that is precisely why you need a spell in the gym."

"Why? To kill me?"

"It won't kill you."

"It'll bore me to death, if nothing else."

"Granted, it doesn't set me alight either," admitted David. "What about cycling? I've got a bike, and I quite like that."

"Piles," said Laz, cryptically.

"Five-a-side then," suggested David.

"Bollocks!" replied Laz with feeling. "Anyway, it's staring you in the face, man. You've enjoyed coming here with me today haven't you?"

"Yes, it's fantastic. There's something quintessentially English about sitting outside the old pavilion with a cup of tea, watching the cricket. I love it. Grass-stained cricket whites, the reassuring clunk of leather on shin-bone, Panama hats, gentle applause, lovely timeless villages, the old scoreboard that nobody can understand, dainty cucumber sandwiches..."

"Yes, okay, I've got the idea. So why not play it yourself?"

"Good question! Well, for a start, the last time I played cricket was at Tipperton Grammar. I was about fourteen, and I was crap at it then. I don't even understand the rules properly, and I'm scared of folks throwing lumps of solid wood at me at speeds of eighty-

4

plus miles per hour. How's that for starters?"

Laz smiled. "*Nobody* understands the rules. It doesn't matter. Cricket would be perfect for you, Dave. It's a bit more genteel for a man of your advanced years than, say football, and, as you said just now; you love all that traditional stuff. As for lumps of wood, well, I admit it *looks* dangerous, but you wear lots of protection — pads and helmets and gloves and so forth. I reckon you should see someone after the game and apply to join Enville. They might give you a run out in the seventh team reserves or something, or maybe the Under Tens. You'll love it."

"Hang on," interrupted David, "what do you mean *you*? What happened to *us*?"

"Oh, I can't get involved," explained Laz airily, dismissing the suggestion with a regal wave of the hand, "I've got a bit of arthritis in my wrist. I couldn't hold the bat properly, or bowl, for that matter. No, you go ahead."

"But what are you going to do, as part of our agreed Middle-of-the-Year Resolution?"

"Did we agree? I don't remember agreeing."

"Well, not in so many words, but you should give me moral support and join in. I reckon you should give up smoking, for a start."

Laz choked on his Benson and Hedges King Sized.

"Sod off! It's the only pleasure I get. It helps with my stress levels, it..."

"Will probably kill you before you're fifty. You'll be totally stress-free then." David fixed Laz with a level stare. "A wager, Laz. You pack in smoking by the end of the cricket season, and I have to knock my first fifty in a proper game. The loser pays a forfeit."

"Such as?"

"Something cringeworthy maybe? Something you'd rather not do?"

"Such as?"

"Dunno. Let me sleep on it."

Their conversation was once more interrupted by a magnificent six that had the oldest member scurrying for cover behind the tea urn.

"Fair enough," said Laz reluctantly. "Oh, by the way, don't think I'm being personal, but you're losing your hair."

"I'm so glad you pointed it out, Laz. I wouldn't have known had you not informed me."

"Least I could do for an old friend," smiled Laz. "You see, I might be a big, fat bastard, but I can always diet, whereas...."

"I'll fetch the teas," growled David.

Chapter 2

A Steep Learning Curve

"This is Spud from the Under Thirteens," said Barry Suggs, the first team captain. "We'll start here in the nets, David, just to see what you can do. Spud will bowl a couple of slow deliveries at you, and I just want you to defend the wicket, rather than try and knock the balls for six. Understood?"

David nodded nervously. It was all very humiliating, having to play with a little overweight kid. All the others were training with folks their own age. He took position and stared, blinking into the hot sunshine, while Spud turned his back and lumbered away slowly to the far distant spot where he would begin his run up. This gave David a much needed burst of confidence. The lad seemed to be lame, and in a poor state. If the ball actually reached his bat, it would be a miracle. In spite of this, David began to breathe heavily, his head pounding with the heat inside his helmet, his screwed-up eyes watching every movement of Spud's body.

Spud turned, and began trundling up towards the quaking batsman. What had started as a slow trot soon became a mighty thundering run, and by the time he arrived at the line, he must have been doing fifty miles per hour. Dust clouds gathered behind his sturdy frame, before he took off, leaving the parched ground like a jumbo jet. There was a flash as his arm turned, followed by the clatter of ball upon wicket. David glanced behind him. The stumps were in disarray, and the bails had leapt through the green mesh of the nets and were perched at jaunty angles in a fresh pile of horse manure on the other side. He had vaguely seen the ball coming until it got within a few yards of his trembling body. Then it seemed to disappear, just as the Tardis was prone to do, re-assembling inches behind him, just in time to demolish his stumps.

"How is he?" screamed Spud, a little too cockily for David's liking. What had happened to respect for one's elders?

"I thought you said Spud was a slow bowler?" he complained to his new coach.

"He is," replied Barry. "Would you like him to send you something even slower?"

"If it's no trouble."

Barry gingerly retrieved the bails from their malodorous bed of horse droppings and replaced them.

Spud, meanwhile, limped back, polishing the ball on his whites. This time, he allowed himself a very small run up of around three steps, rather than the two miles he had pounded during his initial bombardment. Perhaps, thought David, it would be possible to grind him down eventually. The lad appeared to have no stamina whatsoever, if this latest run-up was anything to go by. He had clearly shot his bolt, and needed to keep off the pork pies.

David adopted his stance, while Spud took his three lumbering steps. This time, he seemed to be throwing the ball out of the back of his hand, so that instead of rocketing towards him as the last one had done, it sailed harmlessly through the air at a snail's pace. Eager to make amends, David stepped forward and took a mighty sweep at the ball, intending to pole-axe the horse in the neighbouring field, whom he suspected of fouling the area behind the nets. The ball bounced just as David was about to hit it, and then a peculiar thing happened. Instead of coming up at the bat, it seemed to develop a mind of its own: either that or some person unknown was directing it via a remote-control console. Veering sharply to the left, it avoided David's wild sweep completely, once more removing the evil-smelling bails.

David glanced behind him, his face flushing red inside his sweaty helmet.

"How is he?" screamed Spud.

"Plumb!" smiled Barry proudly. "Turned a mile!"

"Bollocks!" sighed David, under his breath.

"Can I bowl some fast ones at him now?" asked Spud eagerly. David blanched beneath his tan.

"Not till I've worked on him," replied Barry, flinging a brotherly arm around David's deflated round shoulders.

"We have work to do," he frowned. "For a start, this is a bat, not a bloody scythe. You'll never hit anything, the way you're holding the bugger. First we'll work on that, and defending these here stumps. Killing the horse doesn't come till lesson twelve."

* * *

"Don't feel downhearted," said Barry, back at the clubhouse. "It's much harder than it looks, and you've never had a go before. Young Spud is the Under Thirteens' Captain and plays for the County too. He's played since he was seven, and his dad played for Worcester. I bet he can't paint pictures like you though, David. Everyone's different. Besides, you played a few good defensive strokes, once you'd recovered from that one in the knackers."

"I had extra incentive to do so after that," David winced. You're right though. It's in young Spud's blood, and it's all totally new to me. I don't know any cricket terms, or the rules or anything. It's all so complicated."

"Chess on grass, David, chess on grass. I've got a good book I can lend you, which explains all the basic terms, techniques and so on, and it's also got a good section on the history of the game. A sort of bluffer's guide, if you like. And I can lend you a video about The Ashes, if you'd like to watch it."

"I'm ashamed to say, I don't even know what The Ashes are," admitted David. "You see, I'm hopeless."

"Bloody hell, I've got my work cut out with you. And you reckon you've had a bet with Laz that you can knock a fifty by the end of the season? Do you realize how hard that is? You may as well hand him the money now."

"Not so. Can you imagine him packing in the fags? I knew what I was doing."

Barry considered this. "I'd say you're both on a hiding to nothing, but if you want, I'll try and get you up to scratch, providing you promise to listen. Meanwhile, let me tell you about The Ashes. Get a round in and pin your ears back. I can't stand to have such ignorant buggers around me. Here beginneth your cricketing education, young man."

* * *

David was in the kitchen, reading his borrowed cricket book. His wife, Suzanne, was drinking tea and studying the Daily Mail.

"Did you know that Australia beat England for the first time ever in England on the 28th and 29th of August, 1882?" he asked her.

"What?"

"England — beaten by Australia. One spectator dropped dead and another bit chunks out of his umbrella handle."

"What did he do that for?"

10

"Because Australia beat England."

"Was it the man who ate his umbrella that dropped dead?" asked Suzanne, cutting out a token that promised her the chance to win a dream cottage in Devon.

"No, that was another bloke. Then, the next year, when England beat Australia *in* Australia, some ladies from Melbourne burnt one of the bails and sealed the ashes in an urn. This woman gave it to a bloke called Ivo Bligh, and he married her."

What, just because she gave him a tea urn?"

David glanced across at his wife with a look of pity, as she finished trimming her token neatly and popped it into an envelope with the words 'Holiday Cottage' written on it in her naïve, childlike handwriting.

"Old Ivo gave it to the MCC, and it's been at Lord's ever since."

"That's good."

"It's only a crappy old thing, but it's become the most treasured trophy in sport, apparently."

"They're giving away a full Wedgwood tea service next," said Suzanne, engrossed.

"Four and a half inches tall — that's all it is. Mad isn't it?"

"It's blue with a gold rim."

"It isn't. It's a dirty brown colour."

"What is?"

"The Ashes. Have you heard a bloody word I've said?"

"Of course!" said Suzanne. "New Zealand played with England and a player died because he chewed his umbrella. They cremated him and now his body is kept at the House of Lords in a tea urn."

11

"Yes, that's it, dear."

David sighed heavily and continued reading his book.

"Shall we pop down the Merry Hill centre soon? I've got to buy a cricket bat and some whites, and while we're there, I might get you that Rolex for your birthday."

"Yes! When can we go?"

"You bloody heard that all right!" he moaned, dropping his borrowed book onto the kitchen table with a thump.

Coincidentally, David had been discussing 'Female Selective Hearing Syndrome' only the day before with his old friend, as they watched the cricket. Laz had returned from the pavilion with two cups of tea and a distracted air, to ask, apropos of nothing, if Suzanne was prone to ignoring whole chunks of David's conversation. When queried as to the reason behind his outburst, Laz seemed to open his heart, confessing that most, if not all of his output was largely ignored by Annie, his darling wife. He then proceeded to expound his theory on why this often happened.

"Women," he began, chewing thoughtfully on a chocolate digestive, "are similar to dogs."

David thought this something of a sweeping statement and sought to intervene, but was waved down by Laz, who hated to be interrupted in mid flow.

"If you stood in my kitchen and tried to engage my Labrador in conversation, I fear that he would be less than attentive. You could chat about the weather or the price of fish, for example, and he would adopt a glazed look. However, if your conversation included the key words 'dinner' or 'walk' at any point, you would note a marked change in his demeanour. His tail would wag, and he might even let out an excited bark. It is exactly the same with women, except for the fact that they are attuned to different words, such as 'handbag', 'shoes', 'sunglasses' and 'new dress'. Everything else we say goes right over their heads, I'm afraid."

David prided himself on his spirit of fairness. Perhaps, he reasoned, this was merely a defence mechanism on Annie's part, to help her cope with Laz's inane and ceaseless chatter. However, this didn't explain why Suzanne often employed exactly the same technique on him, when his own conversation was never less than sparkling, informative and enlightening. Maybe, he reluctantly concluded, Laz's theory had been perfectly correct after all.

"And not only do they all suffer from F.S.H.S., they are devious, my friend," continued Laz, warming to his theme, "and I'll provide evidence. Has Suzanne ever suddenly, for no apparent reason, passed comment on an item of your clothing, by any chance?"

"In what way?"

"For example, she might say, 'I've just been going through the shirts in your wardrobe, and the collars are frayed on a couple of them.' "

The look of recognition spread across David's childlike countenance. "Funny you should mention that, but she does, yes! I must admit, I'm quite flattered when she does that – you know - takes an interest. I wouldn't have a clue what's going on in her wardrobe, or what's wearing thin. I suppose they're more sensitive than us men."

Laz looked up at the heavens in despair and sighed heavily.

"You poor, misguided, gullible sap! Hook, line and sinker, checkmate!"

"What, if anything, are you on about?" frowned David.

"I bet she suggested a trip to Merry Hill to buy you a couple of new shirts, did she not?"

"Yes, she did actually."

"And I bet she played the attentive wife, helping you try things on and telling you what suited you."

13

"S'pose so!"

"And when you left the shop with your two shirts, that was when she delivered the killer blow."

"Eh?"

"Did she or did she not then turn round to you and say, 'Well, *you've* had a couple of new shirts, so I'm going to get me those Ray Bans'?"

David's jaw dropped. "That's uncanny! How did you know that?"

"Ray Bans was a lucky guess, to be honest. A stab in the dark based on the psychology of the individual. It could have been a new swimsuit, a handbag or whatever. If they show an interest in buying you a token something or other, it's only to pave the way for a guilt-free purchase of their own. There's *always* a hidden agenda with women. That's why they're called women, if you follow me." Laz sipped his tea with a flourish and rested the case for the prosecution.

David was aghast. It was as if the mists had cleared from his eyes in re. the opposite sex. If they could employ these devious shirt-buying tactics against their loved ones in order to procure top-of-the-range sunglasses, what else were they capable of? He began to mentally trawl through his recent sexual encounters, searching for suspected fake orgasms.

* * *

Back in the kitchen, David eyed Suzanne with a level stare as she grabbed her handbag – animated and enthused for the first time that morning.

"While we're down there," she smiled, "you should buy some

14

new socks. The ones in your drawer are full of holes."

David just grabbed his car keys, pretending not to hear.

Chapter 3

A Dastardly Plot

Enville Cricket Club was full to overflowing thanks to the arrival of the Australians. The Canberra Convicts were a touring side, made up from a couple of local teams in the Capital Territory area. It was their stated intention, during their prolonged stay, to play at as many small village venues as possible, whilst simultaneously trying to drink every single pint of lager in the Mother Country. It was an enterprise doomed to fail, but they were intent on giving it their best shot. The trip to England also held another, almost greater attraction. It had been organized to coincide with the visit of a considerably more eminent team to those shores, namely, the Australian national side, which was due to play the first of the 1993 Ashes test series on the fourth of June at Old Trafford. Tickets were hard to come by, but they were determined to catch at least a couple of matches before they flew home.

The Convicts' team, it was fair to say, had members of all ages with mixed cricketing abilities. There were some players who were still in their thirties, a few in their forties, and one who was fifty-nine if he was a day. Half of them, when sober, just about knew one end of the bat from the other, and the others made up for their lack of finesse with a wonderful enthusiasm and zest for the game, alcohol and life in general.

The tour didn't get off to the best possible start with a heavy defeat in the Home Counties, to an Old Age Pensioners' Eleven. Never ones to dwell on their shortcomings, the Convicts blamed their trouncing on jet-lag, and staggered on to Somerset, where they placed the blame for the next heavy defeat (at the hands of a ladies team) squarely on the potent nature of the Farmhouse Scrumpy. Those not temporarily blinded, seriously addled or both by the lethal brew gamely proceeded north to Birmingham, promising to catch up with the casualties, once they had been released from the local psychiatric wing.

Next stop was Sparkbrook, where they encountered a largely Asian team that boasted three superb spin bowlers, two demon fast bowlers and a handful of batsmen who wouldn't have looked out of place in the national side. After winning the toss - the only thing they had won so far - the Aussies chose to field. Following a pyrotechnic display of batting, the Sparkbrook side declared on five hundred and sixty-two for three, which caused the deflated Convicts to seek solace in the pavilion bar. After a brief lunch break, during which they unwisely decided to forego the cucumber sandwiches in favour of liquid sustenance, the opening batsmen fell out onto the pitch in high spirits, eager to stamp their authority on the game with some big-hitting, boundary-pummeling stuff - the kind of thing they'd seen Ian Botham do no end of times after a night on the town.

After toiling for just under an hour in the field, they had registered a first innings total of thirty two, all out. This score, however, was a little misleading - they were actually much worse than that. At one point, one of the thirstier batsmen had made an official complaint to the umpire about one of the Sparkbrook bowlers. The gist of his argument appeared to be that the Asian player looked too much like Diana Ross and was throwing three balls at a time – neither of which, he insisted, was allowed in the rule book.

Their tails now firmly between their legs, the deflated and

demoralized Convicts pressed on into the Black Country for an encounter with Cradley Heath Cricket Club, and it was here that their fortunes took a turn for the better.

The Cradley Heath men had decided to go out on a team-building curry night before their first ever international match, and had succumbed to a nasty bout of food poisoning. On the day of the game, most of the players looked greener than the grass stains on their trousers, but to their credit, none of them wanted to let the others down, so battle commenced.

The Convicts (who had miraculously remained abstemious to a man in an attempt to snatch just one victory before they eventually flew home) batted first, but struggled with the run-rate. The Cradley Heath men, in marked contrast, seemed to be getting the runs with consummate ease, as a result of which they hardly ever managed to field eleven men on the pitch at the same time. The game was eventually declared an honourable draw. Things, The Convicts felt, were beginning to look up.

It was with this newfound spirit of optimism that the Great Australian Cricket Circus rolled into Enville. There to meet and greet them was that most generous and gregarious of ambassadors, Larry Homer – Laz to his friends.

Laz was a sociable animal. He liked nothing better than to be surrounded by a group of highly-spirited friends and a few gallons of alcohol. It was here that he was in his element. He introduced himself to everyone, and ferried tray after tray of lager from the clubhouse, in an attempt to make the Antipodeans feel at home. He enthralled them with the tale of how David had once been found, naked and covered in toothpaste in the girls' dorm at a Youth Hostel in Stow on the Wold. He regaled them with stories of how a nineteen-year-old David had ended up penniless and dressed in women's attire in Florence, and he mesmerized them with the saga of David's Mini Clubman, and how it was destroyed by the Wolverhampton police in a controlled explosion. The

Australians, enthralled, regaled and mesmerized in the order named, were loving every minute of it. Meanwhile, David looked on from a discreet distance in horror, making a mental note to disembowel Laz with a Samurai sword immediately after the event.

"There he is now, just behind that shrub," laughed Laz, calling David over to meet his newfound best buddies. "Dave! Come and meet the Aussies!"

"Yeah, g'day, yer mad bastard!" smiled the big ugly one with the Mel Gibson mullet hairdo. "Christ man! You're a bloody nutter and no mistake. Let me buy yer a beer."

David reluctantly sidled over, politely refusing the offer of alcohol on the grounds that he never usually bothered before nine-thirty a.m. Miraculously, he was spared further embarrassment by the arrival of the Australian team captain, who announced that his boys had won the toss and had elected to bat. Downing their pints in one gulp, they scurried off to attend the team tactics talk and prepare, with one embittered player complaining that they'd never knowingly employed tactics before, and they were eating into his drinking time.

"Why is it," began David, once the commotion had subsided and order was restored to its throne, "that all your anecdotes tend to feature my public humiliation, in one form or another?"

Laz looked hurt. "Well, I don't want the buggers taking the piss out of *me* do I? Besides, I can't help it if you're always getting into weird situations. You must admit, you do attract them."

Try as he might, David couldn't disagree. Weird situations stuck to him like iron filings to a magnet. He decided to change the subject.

"I joined the cricket club, by the way. I took the plunge, paid my subs and did some net practice on Saturday afternoon."

"Fantastic! How did you get on then?"

"It's early days, but I enjoyed it, once I'd got over the sheer fright of having the equivalent of a large cobble thrown at me at speeds approaching Mach Nine."

"Laz winced. "I think I'd be frightened of copping one in the knackers."

"We cricketers are used to such things," smiled David, waving a dismissive hand. "Apart from having testicles that now resemble over-ripe plums, there were few side effects, once the initial three and a half hours of gut-wrenching, searing, unspeakable pain had subsided, and I was able to breathe on my own without the respirator."

"Oh dear! And I suppose you have to be careful with your precious hands too. Come to think of it, it's maybe not the best sport for a man who is one of Britain's premier artists and restorers of old masterpieces."

"You're too kind. Modesty forbids me to agree with you of course. Actually, it's Europe's, not just Britain's, but we'll let it pass. No, you're right. I must be careful. I don't think I'm cut out for 'silly mid on'. I'll ask them if I can stand by the boundary I think. Anyway, no sign of my knocking a half-century just yet, I'm afraid to say. What about you? I note you're still smoking!"

"Ah!" replied Laz, "But I have cut down. I'm seeing a hypnotist on Friday and she reckons she can cure my addiction."

"Well done!" David was impressed. He'd presumed that Laz would have forgotten all about their wager. "So where did you come by her, Yellow Pages?"

Laz placed his beer on a mat and leant towards his friend.

"No, but here's the strange thing. I was chatting to that little fat fellow with no eyebrows at the bar the other day – the one who keeps the wicket in good nick and cuts the grass – Dick Nibbells."

"No one is called Dick Nibbells."

"*He* is. Anyway, he's got a twin sister called Nancy who runs a part-time hypnotism business from a tiny little first floor office in Stourbridge High Street, and she specializes in phobias, addictions and so on."

"Nancy Nibbells? It's getting worse. What were their parents thinking?"

"And he reckons his twin sister can cure me in a couple of sessions."

David pondered this. "Are they identical twins, I wonder?"

Laz sighed and shook his head, making his double chin wobble disconcertingly. "You are the most talented chap I know. You are a sought-after artist, a decent guitarist and you got a good degree at University. It amazes me how you can be so unworldly and stupid sometimes. They are brother and sister, dimwit. How can they be bloody identical?"

"Oh yeah! Sorry. So have you met her yet, this Nancy Nibbells? I bet she intends to take you under and then have her way with you. I've heard of that before, you know. You'll wake up with no memory of it, but your todger will probably feel sore and used when you get home - you mark my words."

"If she *does* look like a female version of Dick, hypnotism is the only way she'll ever get any," agreed Laz. "Look, I'm pragmatic about these things. If I'm unconscious she can do what she likes, as long as she cures my smoking problem. I shall expect a discount though, if she uses me for sex."

David excused himself from this latest in-depth philosophical discussion to visit the lavatory. He'd been dying to relieve himself for ages, and all of a sudden, he could wait no longer. He dashed into the rather dismal, sweaty-smelling facilities and made a beeline for the end cubicle. With his private parts in their current swollen and discoloured state, he was even more loath than usual to flash them around at the common trough.

As he sat, cross-eyed and ecstatic with relief, he gingerly examined his battered organ, worried about his chances of fathering more children. A wry smile crossed his lips as he remembered the old joke about asking the doctor to reduce the pain but keep the swelling. It was a wonder Laz hadn't already used it, once he'd become cognizant of the nature of David's injury.

It was during this period of quiet contemplation that he heard the doors of the remaining two cubicles swing open almost simultaneously, followed by the footsteps of persons unknown stepping inside. There were the customary sounds of belts being unbuckled and zips unzipping, along with the usual explosive bursts of wind. The two men appeared completely unashamed of their trumpeting, and even seemed to be displaying a certain pride in their scatological achievements. Quite soon they were actually working together, as would a northern brass band, but the results were less Brighouse and Rastric than Shithouse and Gastric.

David, always amused by such simple slapstick comedy, sat in total silence, biting his lip and enjoying every pungent outburst. It put him in mind of the music from the Hovis advert played on whoopee cushions. Sublime, but mercifully brief, the tenants to his right concluded their ensemble piece without so much as an apology, and then one of them gave tongue.

"Christ mate! Better out than in, I say."

The words were spoken in a strong Australian accent.

"It's all this gassy Pom beer!" complained the Second Trumpet. "Are we alone?"

"Dunno mate," the Lead Trombone replied, "Anyone here?"

David panicked. He wasn't sure how to react to such a forthright and unexpected enquiry, and so he wisely, or perhaps foolishly, elected to say nothing. The first Australian continued.

"Anyway, Brett - as I was saying. I'm not leaving here without 'em. Maurice J. Trilby is one tough cookie, and what he wants, he gets."

"You're not bloody kidding, mate," agreed the Trumpet, "but stealing them is another thing. He's asking the impossible."

"They don't belong in England, Brett mate. They belong in Australia - everybody knows that. They were spirited away without consent. I know it sounds impossible, but I really believe we can do it. Trilby is paying us a lot of money to pull this off, and this tour gives us the perfect opportunity to do it. We've got a bit of time to finalize the plan, so relax. We hit London again on the sixteenth of June. That's the day we do the deed. If all goes well, we'll be on the plane home a few days later. It's a shame that we'll have to miss the other test matches, but I reckon we'll need to make ourselves scarce after that. Hanging around the old Mother Country for weeks afterwards wouldn't be the smartest thing we'd ever done, would it?"

"Agreed, but what if it all goes pear-shaped, Mervin? And where do we hide the bloody urn?"

"It won't *go* pear-shaped, mate. The thing's only small – we can hide it in a shoe for God's sake, and it won't look suspicious on any X Ray either. I'm telling you straight, mate. I'm not going back to Oz without the ashes."

Chapter 4

David, Laz and Vincent

Laz drove through the open five-barred gates and crunched across the gravel drive. He parked his Porsche 911 neatly next to David's gleaming Mercedes convertible and sat for a while, studying his surroundings. David had done very well for himself, with his large, detached barn conversion and specially built art studio. The two friends had come a long way since they first met, and formed a rock band together in the seventies. David was a penniless, long-haired art student then, while Laz was a frizzy-haired hippy car mechanic with a penchant for eye-liner and stack-heeled boots. He glanced at himself in the rear-view mirror and cringed at the memories that flooded back. He became aware of his gently throbbing head – nothing untoward for Laz, it had to be said. If his head didn't throb, it meant that he hadn't consumed bucket loads of wine and spirits the night before, and if he hadn't, then he wasn't Laz. The throbbing sensation therefore, was reassuring. It confirmed who was staring back at him.

There was a time when Laz enjoyed staring at mirrors, but nowadays, he tended to avoid them. For a man who was, in spirit, eternally the young rock star with a lifestyle to match, it was uncomfortable having to be reminded of the ravages of time. He smoothed the loose grey straggly hairs above his ears and examined his pigtail. A wry smile formed on his lips as he savoured the contradiction of his and David's appearances. The successful businessman with a large factory should, by rights, have been sporting a short, neat hairdo and a suit, whereas the bohemian artist should surely have been the one with the old T shirt and pigtail. Laz didn't mind having a businessman's house, car and income, but it was a step too far to wear the uniform. Frank Zappa would have turned in his grave, had he seen his greatest fan wearing a three-piece suit and tie, and more importantly, had he been dead.

David, for his part, hated art students, even when he had been one, but he also realized, once he'd left college, that artists were not given the respect they deserved if they *looked* like artists. To this end, he had cut his hair short and often wore light linen suits and ties, or cream Oxford bags with brogue shoes. This gave him the 'Our Man in Panama' look which appealed to him no end. If the truth were known, he actually quite enjoyed being mistaken for a businessman, and was always quoting Gustave Flaubert's memorable line; 'Be regular in your life so that you may be violent and original in your work'. This made David sound like an intellectual, which he wasn't. He hadn't a clue who Gustave Flaubert was or what he did, and had found the quote in, of all things, Frank Zappa's autobiography, a book lent to him by Laz. Where Frank had found the quote was not recorded.

Laz would often call by the Day residence for a quick cup of tea and a packet of chocolate digestives, if he was in the area. Today, however, was different, and a little perplexing. He had received a strange, jittery phone call from David that morning, asking him to pop in as soon as he could manage to. When Laz had probed his friend for more details, he was told that it was a matter of some importance, and not discussable on the phone. Intrigued, he'd jumped straight into the 911 and headed over at once.

No sooner had he opened the car door, than David was striding purposefully across the gravel to meet him. They walked around the side of the barn together to David's beautiful new studio building, and climbed the outside stairs to the top floor, where

25

David restored his pictures.

Generally, no one was allowed into David's inner sanctum except for Laz and Suzanne (for cleaning purposes) and both had sworn an oath of secrecy. For the average fine artist, this would have sounded paranoid in the extreme, but David was not your average artist, and there was good cause. Some of the works of art that fleetingly passed through the place were literally worth millions. Allowing his friend anywhere near the place might have seemed, to the casual observer, like foolhardiness, given Laz's gregarious nature and predilection for conversation with total strangers over a pint or seven. In this case, the casual observer, whoever he or she might be, would have been wrong to cast aspersions. Laz knew precisely what David's business meant to him, and had sworn a solemn oath not to divulge any information about what he witnessed at the studio. He would gleefully spread false rumours about David being a transvestite, or anything else that popped into his child-like mind, but he knew where the line was, and when not to cross it. He and David hadn't exactly slashed each other's palms with a pen-knife and pressed their bloodied hands together, but a sacred oath it was, and David trusted his old pal as he would trust his own mother.

David Day had cut his teeth in the world of advertising as an illustrator, and had served a long apprenticeship. He was well-respected throughout England as a painter of detailed, craftsman-like pictures, which graced the covers of magazines, decorated postage stamps and record sleeves, and advertised just about every product from marmalade to Rolls Royces. The problem was, he was too good at it for his own well being, and didn't know how to say no. This had resulted in a period of intense pressure that had made him ill and catapulted him to the brink of nervous collapse. After a bleak day one December, during which he'd crawled back to bed, pulled a pillow over his head and cried like a baby, Suzanne had made a few decisions that David was woefully unable to make for himself, and told virtually all of his clients to take a running jump. She could manage without the car, or the holidays, or even the house, but neither of them could manage without David being of sound mind, and so he was persuaded to commence a complete mental clear-out and start afresh. Once this awkward, desolate period had passed, they talked at length about what would make him happy. He chose restoration.

At the tender age of eleven, he had shown a rare talent for copying many different artistic styles, and would often sit for hours, drawing bank notes in minuscule detail with his thirteen-colour biro, or ageing paper with tea, prior to copying fusty old manuscripts with his quill pen.

At the age of nineteen, the talented but naïve art student was persuaded to forge a Monet and a Botticelli for a crook by the name of Lord Hickman, which resulted in farce, when no one, including David, could quite remember which were the originals and which were the fakes. Over the years, David had honed his skills, and after a fortuitous meeting with the curator of the National Gallery, he was offered freelance work as an art restorer. He quickly rose to the top of his tree, and before long was restoring torn Titians, ripped Renoirs and vandalized Vermeers.

David's work involved lots of travelling, because often the works of art had to be repaired or restored *in situ*, particularly if they were church frescos. The Post Office tended to take a dim view when asked to deliver a complete fifteenth century convent wall scantily protected by bubble-wrap and brown paper with second class stamps attached, especially if it was sent recorded delivery. If the art restorer wasn't in, the poor postman had to lug it back to the depot.

When David was a younger man, a month in Prague lying face-up on a rickety scaffold seemed like a good idea, but not any more. He'd been there, done that and got the paint-spattered T shirt. Now that he had a nice house, a lovely wife and a young daughter, he preferred to spend as much time as he could with them, not hanging upside down from a roof like some kind of artistic bat, with spiders crawling down his neck and paint blobs dripping into his eyes. Nowadays, though he was still occasionally lured away to Italy if the money was right, he liked to restore paintings in frames that could be couriered to his studio and couriered back again when completed. His insistence on working at home whenever possible had not gone down big with some of his major clients, however. They worried about the security angle. A Renoir may well have been easier to handle than a convent wall, but the National Gallery still baulked at the idea of dealing with the Post Office.

"Do you wish to send this Renoir insured?" the imaginary assistant would enquire.

"Certainly!" the imaginary National Gallery director would reply.

"I see. Are the goods worth more or less than two hundred pounds?"

"A tad more actually. I would say twenty million."

"I may have to check this with my supervisor, if you don't mind."

David's reasoning was thus: his studio was equipped with every little item that he might need in the course of a repair, whereas, if he travelled to the gallery in question, it was possible that he could be desperate for a squirt of - for the sake of argument - Underpainting White, only to realize that he'd left it in the drawer by the old sink. In fairness, he had fleshed out his argument a little more than that when trying to convince them of the need to work at home, but there lay the nub. He also tried to explain that constant travel and lack of contact with his family made him stressed and fretful, and in that condition he was unlikely to do his best work. This was all fine and dandy, came the counter-argument, but what about security? Was his house, they enquired snootily, one of those hippy-style communes where people in kaftans wandered in, and having done so, wandering out again with masterpieces under their arms? Did David sometimes leave the door wide open and disappear down the local shops for a bottle of milk, wrapped up in some private fantasy or daydream of artistic creation? It wouldn't be long, argued the galleries, before the shadier half of his village had Canalettos and Constables hanging above their fireplaces next to the official school photo in the blue cardboard window mount.

In order to pacify his clients and quell their fears, David spent an awful lot of money on state-of-the-art alarm systems, shutters and locks, inspiring Laz to christen it 'The Fortress of Solitude' (which showed what kind of reading *he* did).

* * *

David unlocked the door and walked in, followed by a rather shaky-looking Laz, who seemed to be suffering from an attack of vertigo after climbing the steps. Once inside, he made a bee-line for the comfy old leather chesterfield and slumped into it, holding his brow, as if to prevent the two halves of his skull from coming apart.

"Serves you right!" frowned David. "I thought those Aussies could drink, but Jeez!"

"It was a great day though," said Laz, "and what a great result too. I've never heard of a team declaring on twenty-six for four before."

"No," replied David. "I'm no expert, but aren't you supposed to declare when you have reached an unassailable lead?"

"Normally, but I think they declared because they'd given up all hope of getting anywhere and it was just eating into their allotted drinking time. I reckon that's one of those great cricket statistics that'll end up in the Guinness Book of Records or something. The opening Enville pair put that many on the scoreboard in about four minutes and the game was over. I've never seen anything like it. A whole game of cricket played in under half an hour. The Enville captain appealed for a second innings, just to make a longer game of it, but their bloke just got all maudlin and kept saying, 'what's the bladdy point mate? We're total shit!' I felt a bit sorry for them, I must admit. I thought Australia was renowned for its cricketers, so I don't know where they got that lot from. Nice blokes though. I've got a couple at my place now, sleeping it off."

"How's that woman that does the cricketers' teas?" asked David, his face the picture of concern.

"Still in hospital, I'm afraid, but I think they're going to let her out this afternoon."

"I bet they couldn't do that again if they tried a thousand times," mused David, trying his damnedest not to laugh.

"No," agreed Laz, also keeping a lid on his emotions in case his head split in two. "To hit a six like that was impressive enough, but to get it to go through a tiny, open kitchen window without touching the sides was remarkable."

"Yes, and normally that large tub of frozen ice-cream wouldn't have been there, of course. That's the strange thing."

"There's some weight in a full tub of ice-cream too. Pauline buys the big industrial-sized ones from Iceland, because she can get twenty-six portions out of them, which means that the two umpires and the scorers can have one as well."

David was puzzled. "But how come the tub was on top of the fridge-freezer, and how come Pauline was under it? Isn't that a fundamental role reversal, vis-à-vis the usual and accepted positioning of tea-lady and freezer compartment?"

"What?"

"You know what I'm trying to say."

"Sort of. Apparently, she was cleaning out the freezer compartment, with a view to depositing some vol-au-vent cases in there, and had temporarily left the aforementioned tub on top of the fridge-freezer, while she rummaged beneath - no doubt scraping away at the solitary prawn that had become frozen within the ice, like some modern-day woolly mammoth. It was then that Barry Suggs let fly with his magnificent hook shot and all hell broke loose. The club secretary found her spark out with a half-ton block of Butterscotch on the back of her neck. He was extremely agitated, so they say."

"I can understand that. If it had defrosted, just think of the waste."

"Exactly! Anyway, she was knocked out cold, if you'll excuse the pun, but she's recovering now, I think. The doctors at Russell's Hall told her she was concussed, so she's taking a couple of days off when she's released. Suggs went to see her, as he felt partly responsible, and she kept calling him Ernest, which is her late husband's name."

David looked puzzled. "I didn't know her husband was dead."

"He's not; he plays in the third team. He's just always late, hence his nick-name. The point I was making was that she's confused at the moment, that's all. Anyway, you didn't call me over here to chat about yesterday's game. What's up?"

David closed the front door and pulled up a chair. "I heard something yesterday that would chill your blood, old pal."

Laz was all ears. He followed his mother for that. He was also listening attentively. "Go on."

"I was in the loo, when two of those Aussies came in. They sat themselves next to me in the cubicles, and began plotting, thinking they were alone. You're not going to believe this."

31

"What, they were gay?"

"Oh please! They were plotting to steal something – a national treasure, no less."

"The Queen Mother? They'll never get her through customs."

David gave him one of his looks. "Laz, I'm being deadly serious. The Aussies are planning to steal The Ashes."

"What!"

"The Ashes! They plan to smuggle them back to Australia. They're playing a game in London, and that's when they're going to strike. The trophy is being stolen to order for some bloke called Trilby. The same thing happens all the time in the art world. Some fanatic pays millions just to have a real Picasso, even though he can never show it to anyone. They keep them in vaults and just pop down to gloat over them when they need a fix."

At this juncture, David's front door was rapped sharply from without, causing both David and Laz to leap like rocketing pheasants from their seats. "Excuse me," said David. "I'm expecting a delivery."

He opened the door to two men dressed in security guard outfits and batsman-style helmets. They asked him to sign here, here and here, whereupon David signed there, there and there in the order named. They presented him with a small, shallow wooden case and duly left. Suspending the conversation at eleven hundred hours, he excitedly opened the box and with extreme care, removed a framed oil painting.

"My Van Gogh," he smiled, showing it to Laz. "Want to hold it?"

"*That's* a Van Gogh?" asked Laz, his eyes like saucers.

"Yep! Not a great one, but one nevertheless. It's from the National Gallery. Some nutter drew a penis on it with a felt pen, before the burly guards wrestled him to the floor and ripped his head off. See?"

Laz studied the painting. It didn't require an expert's eye to spot the felt-pen penis. It was bang in the middle of a bright yellow cornfield, surrounded by crows.

"Bloody hell, Dave!" he sighed, shaking his head from side to side in sheer disbelief. "You've got a weird job, mate!"

David placed the painting onto an easel and resumed his train of thought. "As I was about to say before Vincent turned up. We've got to do something, such as call the London Police right away, for example, don't you think?"

"Are you pulling my leg?" asked Laz. "Those blokes were just everyday, fun-loving characters - daft as a brush. They're not hardened bloody criminals."

"You're probably right," replied David. "Most of them. Nine of them in fact, but two of them are not just here for the beer or the cricket. Mervin and Brett are here to rob us of our heritage, no less."

"Christ!" gasped Laz. "They're the ones staying at my house!"

Chapter 5

The Note

Laz stood at his kitchen table, reading and re-reading the note that Mervin and Brett had left for him.

"Dear Laz. Sorry we had to blow, mate. Took the liberty of borrowing fifty quid from your tinnie for the train fares, 'cause we missed the tour bus. We know you won't mind, as it's probably small change to a bloke that drives a bloody 911.

Love, the Convicts."

He mouthed a choice expletive and tossed the note back onto the table. It landed face down, as tossed notes are wont to do, at least half of the time, and this drew his attention to more words and a diagram scrawled on the back. The shaky doodle appeared to represent a room with what looked like two doors, with another rectangle running along the longer wall. Within this rectangle were written the misspelt words 'Trophie Cabinett' and two arrows marked the position of 'Sicurity cameras'. Next to the room drawing was a long wobbly line with the word 'Corrider,' and another arrow pointing to 'Reer exit'.

Beneath this hastily constructed diagram were the words, '16th

June. Alarm system off - 4.30 till 6.30'.

Laz immediately snatched the piece of paper from his table and studied the crude map, dialing his friend's number as he did so. David was pacing the floor, eying the felt-tip penis from all angles when the phone rang, causing him to splash half of his cup of tea onto the oak floorboards.

"Dave, you were right about those two," Laz began, dispensing with the usual opening pleasantries, "and I've got the evidence right here. They intend to snatch The Ashes on the sixteenth of June, which is the day before the test match at Lord's. It all fits. The Aussie team is arriving, the ground's buzzing with excitement and everyone's getting ready for the game. The ground staff will be busy busy busy, and maybe they won't have their eye on the ball. Meanwhile, someone on the inside will have bypassed the alarm system, allowing a couple of strictly unofficial, uninvited and unwelcome Aussies in through the back door to do their dirty deed. We have to call the police right away!"

David was kneeling on the floor with the phone wedged against his ear, mopping up the spilt tea with a piece of kitchen roll as he listened. On hearing this spectacular confirmation of his suspicions, his right hand began to tremble, causing the remainder of his tea to meet the same fate as the first half.

"I knew it, I bloody well knew it!" he blurted, almost beside himself with excitement. "Listen, I have to travel to London tomorrow to visit an exhibition. This is perfect timing. I'll try and find out who the top copper is for that area of the city and fix up an appointment. I'll tell them it's of national importance, and I need to speak to him face to face. Meanwhile, I'll pop round as soon as I can and pick up the evidence."

He replaced the receiver and stood biting his nails and gazing out of the window for what seemed like a good ten minutes, but was probably only eight. Eventually he dragged himself out of his

reverie, placed his empty tea mug on the draining board and ran
down to his car.

* * *

David's mind was elsewhere. Normally, he would have been in
his element, wandering around the National Gallery and taking in
the Vermeer exhibition, but on this occasion he was just too full of
nervous energy to appreciate it. He tried to relax in the tea rooms
with a copy of the Daily Mail and a toasted teacake, but every
time he tried to read an article, his eye would bounce from chapter
to chapter, picking out the odd word here and there, without
making any sense whatsoever of what he'd read. He'd wanted Laz
to accompany him on the trip and supply much-needed moral
support, but work commitments and his first session with Nancy
Nibbells had prevented him from doing so.

David nipped thoughtfully at his teacake, trying once more to
make head or tail of the Daily Mail's pearls of wisdom and
enlightenment. He read and re-read the headline to one particular
article, but it was almost as if dyslexia had set in without any prior
warning. Either that or else the prescription for his reading glasses
had suddenly run out.

SHOPLIFTERS PAY-RISE OFFER
REJECTED BY UNIONS

Was he going mad? Shoplifters didn't have unions, surely. He
knew there were lots of them in the Capital, but this was going too
far - he had no idea they were so organized. It was only upon
reading the line for the seventh time that he realized his mistake.
The word was in fact SHOPFITTERS. Either he needed to update

his glasses or else he was just too stimulated and hyper to concentrate on the newspaper. Turning the page and trying to find something simple that he could digest, David smiled wryly as he spotted the Dream Cottage token. Maybe he should tear it out for Suzanne - it would give him something to do to while away the time till his appointment. He took a slurp of tea, which went down the wrong way and left him choking. After a series of dramatic convulsions, he blasted hot, brown fluid across the table towards a rather intense-looking Londoner who was studying his exhibition programme. Apologizing profusely, once he was able to, David vacated the table and glanced nervously at his watch as he made his way to the foyer. He replaced his left hand into the pocket whence it came, and then realized that he still had no idea what time it was. He tried again, this time remembering to actually study the dial. Ten to two - his appointment was at half-past. If he took a slow walk to the tube station, he should arrive at his destination bang on time.

Due to unforeseen circumstances, the exhibition trip had been a short and unfulfilling one, but David did love Vermeer's work, and his own chosen style of painting was quite similar. In fact, so similar that David's old college friend, Dylan, suspected that he might have been suffering from Vermeereal disease. David admired Vermeer's use of light, and the quiet, still peace of his interiors, but on this particular day, even old Johannes couldn't soothe his savage breast. He was burdened with a secret so important to the history of cricket that it was burning away at his insides, and carrying such a heavy load seemed to be playing havoc with his brain, rendering him incapable of clear thought. David really needed to tell what he knew, straight away, to the man who could hopefully do something about it.

At first, it had all seemed like great fun, and he'd even fancied handling the situation himself, just as the heroes of his childhood adventure books would have done. He and Laz could trap the baddies and thwart their dastardly plans, like middle-aged reincarnations of Jennings and Darbyshire. The only trouble was, this wasn't a fictional adventure story about the theft of the school rugger cups, and the thieves didn't wear masks and carry swag bags. David couldn't just give them a jolly good biffing with his cricket bat and then trot off to his dorm for a midnight feast with his chums after lights out. This was real life, where thieves passionately defended their interests with at least kitchen knives and fists full of sovereign rings, if not guns. Nasty, life-threatening wounds were commonplace, as were spells in intensive care, broken noses and splintered teeth. David was too cowardly and good-looking to entertain either of the aforementioned, hence his forthcoming appointment with the boys in blue.

Initially, his phone call to Scotland Yard had been met with a lot of red tape. The receptionist had enquired as to his business, and been told in the most polite way to button it and hand over the Commissioner. This doesn't, as a rule, go down well with Police Receptionists as a class, who, in common with their near-relatives, Doctors' Receptionists, take such responses as a form of slight. They quickly erect obstacles to one's progress; their manner becomes stiff and formal, and window blinds are pulled down with a contemptuous sniff. David, however, was able to win around the lady with his boyish charm, once he realized that she was instrumental in opening the door to the top man, so that quite soon she was eating out of his hand, as would a tame guinea pig or rabbit.

"I would *love* to divulge what I know," he explained earnestly, "but it really is a matter of national security."

Whether a four and a half inch urn full of cinders qualified as a matter of national security was open to debate, but David knew he had to sell it big in order to clear the first hurdle of bureaucracy. It seemed to do the trick, for once the young lady had reminded him that time-wasters could be hanged, drawn and quartered, she put him through to another lady, who introduced herself as the Chief Superintendent's secretary. David, who was trying to hide his disappointment at not landing the Commissioner, repeated his tale, and was rewarded with an appointment at two-thirty p.m., which was when the great man returned from his Cornish pasty and cup of tea at his favourite café round the corner.

After a hot, unpleasant tube ride, during which every care-in-the-community patient, B.O. sufferer and drug addict seemed to crave his attention, David stepped out into the London sunshine, blinking like a confused mole. He strode purposefully in the direction of New Scotland Yard, batting away the various sorry individuals he encountered en-route as they tried to make eye-contact in the vain hope that he could spare them a quid.

He mounted the front steps and entered that legendary home of law enforcement, glancing around in awe as the hairs on his neck respectfully stood to attention. It was, after all, a place where so many notorious crimes had been painstakingly investigated and solved. Now he was about to add his own contribution to their Museum of Criminology - The incredible but true tale of Australia's plot to steal The Ashes. The footnotes of History would disclose that it was foiled by a shy, unassuming artist from near Birmingham, which made him feel inordinately proud. He could see it in his mind's eye, printed on the roll of honour alongside the likes of Dixon of Dock Green, Sherlock Holmes and Hercule Poirot - David Day, the Artist Sleuth. That would be his gimmick – artist by day and detective by night. It had a certain ring to it. All the fictional detectives had to have a trademark, be it a dodgy moustache, a deer-stalker or a glass eye. David would be the artist who sent international gangs and psychopathic gangsters to jail, in-between removing penises from Van Goghs. They might have to alter that bit for the film version, he mused. Maybe some kind of demonic symbol might be more appropriate.

He was awoken from his daydream by a rather pretty female constable who enquired as to his business. David spluttered out his answer and was directed to a row of leather seats, where he was asked to wait. He browsed through the obligatory Yachting

39

Monthly, registering every fiftieth word or so, and cast it down on the small table to his side. Only marginally more interesting was the copy of Loft Insulation World. What was it about doctors' and dentists' waiting rooms, and now New Scotland Yard, he wondered, that caused people to collect such strange magazines? Did people actually subscribe to them and donate them once finished with, or were they published solely for the waiting room coffee table market? Maybe after wading through Porcelain Collectors' Weekly, even an extraction or filling seemed like fun. Perhaps that was the psychology behind it.

Finding no distractions for his troubled soul amongst the magazines, David sought solace in the rack of London attractions on the wall just behind him. Why was it that the Capital had all the best ones, he asked himself. The Tower of London, Buckingham Palace, Downing Street, Madame Tussauds - the list went on. Meanwhile, the rest of the country had to make do with what they could scrape together to attract tourism. Worst of all was Devon. He and Suzanne used to collect awful attractions leaflets just for fun, until they became bored with it. As a result, they had drawers full of such gems as Paperweight World, Button World, Bee World and Garden Gnome World. There was even a place called Pencil World – all establishments that helped pass the grey, rainy days. Fun for all the family! Or you could just hang yourself from the rafters of your damp rented cottage.

"Excuse me!" said a voice in David's right ear.

It had the same effect that, back in Stourbridge, Nancy Nibbell's voice must have had on Laz, as she brought him around from his deep sleep. David let out a startled cry and shot to his feet.

"The Chief Super will see you now, Mister Day. Follow me."

David strode down the corridor, desperately trying to keep up with the young ginger-headed constable, who seemed to be in training for one of those strange Olympic walking races.

"Could you possibly walk a bit slower?" asked David

breathlessly, as they rounded yet another corner at approaching fifteen miles per hour. He was six feet tall and reasonably fit, but this young copper seemed to possess eight-foot telescopic legs.

"Sorry!" he replied, showing no intention whatsoever of reducing his pace, "the boss likes fast walkers."

The words, 'sycophant' and 'brown-noser' jockeyed for pole position in David's brain, but a late spurt by 'twat' produced the winner. The constable came to an unexpected halt, causing David to crash heavily into the back of him, catapulting the policeman's lanky frame into the wall headfirst.

"The Chief Super's Office," announced the rattled young constable, pointing to his right. He gave the door a respectful tap, waited for the voice within to say 'enter' and duly did so.

"Ahem! Mister Day for you, sir," he said, backing out again whilst performing the policeman's version of tugging the forelock. He gestured for David to proceed, and continued his walking race, no doubt keen to shave valuable seconds off his previous time.

The Chief Superintendent sat at his impressive desk, resplendent in his much decorated uniform. As David nervously wandered in, the policeman completed the entry in his diary and looked up at his visitor, smiling broadly.

"Chief Superintendent Trilby," he grinned, "G'day, Mister Day! What can I do for you?"

Chapter 6

An Unexpected Twist

David hadn't expected the Australian accent. It had thrown him, but that was a drop in the ocean compared to how he felt once he'd registered the policeman's name. He stood in the middle of the large room feeling incredibly dizzy, and struggling to come to terms with the situation he found himself in. When the Chief Super asked if David was okay, all David could do was to stand there, gulping in air, like a salmon in a landing net. His wild eyes gawped around the room, coming to rest on a brass name-plate near the front of the policeman's large, polished desk.

Chief Superintendent M. J. Trilby

"Think! Think!" David instructed his deranged brain, whence nothing emerged. It seemed to be paralyzed with fear. What were the chances of coincidence here? Could there possibly be two Australian M.J. Trilbys? David took the chair he had been offered. If he took his time sitting down, it might give him a chance to concentrate his mind. He removed his coat, slowly and theatrically, hanging it on the chair behind him. It was an unusual name. No one else could possibly be named M.J. Trilby – the odds would be enormous. There was no way David could explain why he'd come now. He'd be explaining it to the very man responsible for the plot. There was corruption at the very highest level. Everyone was in on it!

"Are you okay, Mister Day? You look as if you've seen a ghost?"

"Oh, yes, thanks. I felt a bit faint just now. I haven't eaten. I go a bit hyper-what-do-you-call–it. Like diabetics get."

"I'll get you a coffee and a few biscuits."

This bought David a few valuable seconds to marshal his thoughts.

"Time to think. Time to think. Stop saying time to think and actually bloody think, will you? Why on earth would I have come all the way to London to see this bloke, now that I can't mention The Ashes?"

"My secretary will bring us some coffee in a second. Right, Mister Day, if you're up to it, what can I do for you?"

Most days, when David used to be a cartoonist, he'd be asked to come up with ideas for jokes and situations, and quite often, the deadlines were tight. On a good day, the ideas would flow, but occasionally, he would hit a brick wall and suffer the artist's equivalent of writer's block. The deadline would approach at a rate of knots, with David tearing his already thinning hair out and getting nowhere. Then, as the final hour approached, something miraculous would happen. An idea would pop into his mind as if it were a gift from God. He could be washing his hands, riding his bike along the canal towpath and contemplating a watery suicide, or sitting on the lavatory, contemplating his navel, when suddenly – a solution would appear. When asked to explain this phenomenon, David would often use the expression, 'Out of Desperation cometh Inspiration'. It was almost as if he *had* to be up against the wall before some kind of magical release valve

43

would kick in and save his life.

Scrutinized by a quizzical Chief Super, with around four seconds left on the clock before he was booted out into the street for wasting police time, David found himself opening his mouth and speaking.

"My name is David Day, and I do a rather top secret job. Nothing as exciting as yours, I'm afraid, but top secret nevertheless."

The policeman pulled his seat forward, the better to hear what came next.

"I restore valuable paintings at my home. When I say valuable, I mean *really* valuable. Renoirs, Constables and the like, no pun intended."

"And?"

David noticed Brett and Mervin's note poking out of in his trouser pocket. He pushed it back inside.

"I think I've uncovered a plot, to, erm, to erm, steal a Van Gogh from my house."

"I see. And why did you come to me in London, when I understand you're from the Midlands?"

"Ah, good question."

"So answer it."

"Oh right. Well, the, erm, painting belongs to the National Gallery, which is in London."

"I know."

"So I came to the London police."

"Who is responsible for this plot to steal the Van Gogh, Mister Day, may I ask?"

"International art thieves. They're always at it."

"Any in particular that we should know about?"

"Erm, yes. The, erm, Black Penis Gang."

Mercifully, at this juncture, M.J.Trilby's secretary tapped on the door and entered with a silver tray. She set it down carefully on her boss's desk and returned whence she had come. Interview suspended at two-fifty-seven precisely, the policeman and the artist added the necessary milks and sugars, and helped themselves to biscuits. David, swan-like and calm above the water, pedaled furiously beneath it.

"The black what gang? Did I mishear you there?" asked Chief Superintendent Trilby, nibbling his HobNob.

"The Black Penis Gang. They're not officially called that of course – that's just what we art restorers call them. Recently, a restorer friend of mine, erm, Carrivan Innadich – he's, erm, Polish I think – had to restore a Canaletto because someone had drawn a huge black thingy in the middle of St. Mark's Square - that's in Venice - with a felt-tipped pen."

"Excuse me, Mister Day," interjected the officer. "Are you on any form of medication?"

"I know it sounds mad, but hear me out," insisted David, the three brightly-coloured plastic cogs that made up his brain turning furiously, "Spatula Christianson, he's another restorer, gets a Renoir booked in to remove a felt-pen bra and pants that had been crudely added to one of his typical voluptuous nudes, pops to make himself a coffee and hey presto. The Renoir's missing. Don't you see a link here?"

Chief Superintendent Trilby eyed him as a mongoose would a snake.

"Why do all your art restorer chums have weird names?"

David was stung by this slight on his vivid imagination. "With the greatest respect, sir, you are hardly in a position to criticize."

"Point taken. Do continue."

"Well, to me it's offious, obvicer. I'll attempt that again. It's obvious officer. This gang is employing nutters to deface famous works of art so that they then have to be restored. There's only a very small handful of top professionals in the country, so they keep an eye on the security van's movements, or else they have a mole in the museum, and hey presto! The painting's knocked off."

"Is that pre or post penis removal?"

"In an ideal world, post, naturally."

"And you currently have a Van Gogh at your house?"

"Correct! With a big black willy in a cornfield. That's why I reckon I'm next."

"I see. Look, I'm rather busy this afternoon. Leave it with me. Give your name, address and phone number to my secretary before you leave, and we'll make enquiries. How's that?"

"Great!"

"Now if you'll excuse me…."

David rose from his seat and slipped on his coat. He'd been in some tight scrapes in his time, but that was masterful, he thought. Even though he said so himself, the way he'd produced that complete tissue of lies from nowhere, like a rabbit from a hat, was remarkable. The crooked policeman had bought it hook, line and sinker. He shook hands with the Chief Superintendent and strode out of the room, deliberately forgetting to leave his address with the secretary.

One minor detail was niggling him, and casting a cloud over his otherwise buoyant mood. Trilby would now begin to probe into David's allegations and soon discover that they were a complete fabrication. True, there was a Van Gogh with a penis drawn on it.

This was a good start, but the bit about the thefts and his two foreign friends, Carrivan and Spatula were total fabrications. Lord knows where the names came from. They just arrived unannounced courtesy of an over-heated brain. Trilby, if he was worth his salt, would begin by asking the National Gallery if David Day was who he said he was, and then enquire as to the precise nature of the thefts. He would soon discover that there hadn't been any thefts, and as night follows day - or Shite follows Day, as Laz often put it - David would then be receiving irate calls from the Gallery, Scotland Yard or both. Then it would be only a matter of time before he was strait-jacketed, fed through a tube and left to rot in a high security hospital.

The more David thought about the implications of his five minutes of madness, the more his initial slight cloud of concern became the maelstrom from hell. This would need some serious thought on the way home.

As he hurried towards the tube station, he began to see the picture a little more clearly. His situation was serious – that went without saying – but he was forgetting the most important part of the story. It was Trilby who was the criminal, not he. If he could bring the man to justice sooner rather than later, the policeman could be discredited completely. David could then insist that Trilby's counter-accusation against David was nothing more than the ramblings of a criminal madman. The only trouble with this plan was that, until Brett and Mervin tried to steal The Ashes on the sixteenth of June, nothing further could be done. The first test at Old Trafford was imminent, but Lord's was quite a time away. David was walking on egg shells until then.

* * *

In presuming that there could only possibly be one Australian M.J. Trilby, David had been mistaken. There were two.

47

Michael John Trilby, the Chief Superintendent of the Metropolitan Police, Old Scotland Yard, London, was an upstanding pillar of the community. He was born in Sydney, Australia to Gladys and Albert Trilby on the twenty-fifth of January, nineteen-fifty-one, and from an early age, wanted to become a copper, just like his old man. Two years later, the Trilbys were blessed with another boy, Maurice, who had other ideas for a vocation. He liked life on the wrong side of the tracks, and after a few brushes with the law – much to the embarrassment of both his sibling and parents - he settled down to run a 'legitimate' business or two. One consisted of lots of roulette tables, one-armed bandits and hotels, and the other involved pneumatic-breasted naked women gyrating around firemen's poles. Michael and Maurice had never seen eye to eye, but things went from bad to worse when Michael became a chief inspector in Sydney and raided his brother's clubs with alarming regularity. That kind of thing can put a strain on a relationship. Sunday lunches at Trilby Senior's bungalow were terse, silent affairs. Maurice would grumble something about passing the spuds, whereupon Michael would tell him to bloody well get them himself.

It was a blessed relief to all concerned when Michael applied for his post in London, and was accepted. Mrs Trilby had recently shuffled off her mortal coil, and old man Trilby didn't need the extra stress of his two sons bickering every time their paths crossed. Albert Trilby was no fool. He realized that Maurice was a rough diamond, but he loved both sons equally, and they both adored him. It was just that, as is often the case, the two brothers didn't appear to like each other. Separating them by twenty thousand miles or so had seemed like a good idea to old Albert. True, he was left with the more notorious brother, whose business interests and shady friends he could do without, but Maurice, in fairness, was a very loyal and caring son. As Arthur grew old and began to lose his mental faculties, Maurice made sure he wanted for nothing, and even supplied an *au pair* to help his dad around

48

the bungalow. Meanwhile, on the other side of the world, Michael kept in regular contact by blowing huge chunks of his sizeable salary on international phone calls. He also returned to Australia to see Arthur whenever he could, as his father was becoming too frail to travel to England.

This was particularly saddening for Arthur, because, unlike his two disparate sons, he was English. Arthur Trilby had himself been briefly stationed at Scotland Yard, before upping truncheons and jetting away to the Antipodes in search of the good life. It was there that he met Gladys and got married after a whirlwind courtship, which produced baby Michael exactly nine months after the wedding. As a young man, he had become fascinated by cricket, and never missed a game at the nearby Lord's ground. In fact, the only barrier to his happiness down under was the thought of never going to Lord's again, so potent was the ground's magic. As Arthur slowly became a true Australian, and all traces of the Whingeing Pom disappeared, he eased the pain by seeking solace at the Sydney ground, but it wasn't the same somehow. Occasionally, when the money was available, Arthur would fly home to see Michael, and they would sit together in the stands at Lord's watching a game. Michael would see his father's eyes mist over as he remembered the great games of his past. He'd been lucky enough to visit when the Australians were on tour, and confessed to his son that secretly, he'd been rooting for England, in spite of Margaret Thatcher's right-hand man, Norman Tebbit, expressly forbidding it.

The return trips to the Mother Country had dried up, however, due to the overwhelming distances involved, so that Arthur was reduced to catching up with test matches on television. It was during one such match that his voluptuous *au pair*, Kari-Anne, found him in his favourite armchair with a cup of tea in hand, miraculously unspilt but as stone cold as he was, his battle with Alzheimer's finally over.

The funeral had been a strained affair, with Maurice and

Michael bickering as usual. After a brief wake, held at the local cricket pavilion, Michael left Australia for what he imagined was the last time, carrying his father's remains in a little plastic tub. Old Arthur had specifically requested that Michael take them back to England to scatter over the Lord's cricket ground. Unfortunately, due to Arthur's deteriorating mental state, he'd also asked Maurice to scatter them in the bay near the Sydney Opera House.

Chapter 7

An Unforeseen Problem Arises

"So what does she look like then?"

David had just completed his Saturday morning training session and was still in his whites, sipping tea on the clubhouse terrace.

"Well, just like a female version of her brother really. Small, fat and dumpy with ginger, bobbed hair and glasses. It's ever so weird though. I thought, there's no way I'm going to go under, but apparently I did."

"So how does she do it? Does she wave a pendant on a chain in front of your eyes and say, 'You're feeling sleepy'?"

Laz sniffed a superior sniff. "I think you've been watching too many corny films, old pal."

"So what *does* she do then?" asked David.

"She swings this large silver coin on a string from side to side and asks me to relax and think of green fields and so on."

"Oh, right. Nothing like what I suggested then. Silly me. And did you realize you'd gone under or what?"

"Not at all. It's not like falling asleep."

"Strikes me you weren't under at all and she's a bloody con-artist. How much did she charge?"

Laz winced, as he always did when money was mentioned. "Fifty quid per session."

"HOW MUCH?"

"She's got certificates though, remember."

"So have I. I've got a certificate of authenticity that came with a collector's plate that has a fluffy kitten on it, and it's hand-crafted in twenty-four carat gold. Apparently, it's a strictly limited edition of only ten million."

"Go and bollocks!" replied Laz, after a moment of contemplation. "It says she's a member of the Royal something-or-other of Hypnotists, actually."

"I bet she hypnotized you into *thinking* it was a certificate. It was probably her gas bill in a frame. So have you given up smoking yet?"

Laz sheepishly stubbed out his Benson and Hedges King Sized. "Not as such, but she reckons it'll take at least six sessions."

"Six sessions before you've paid for her new kitchen units, you mean? Did you feel any different when she brought you round?"

"Yes, I did actually. I felt lighter,"

"Fifty quid lighter I bet. Anything else?"

"Yes, O Cynical One. I felt peaceful, as if a great weight had been lifted off my mind."

"Off your wallet more like. So how come you're still puffing away?"

Laz gave his friend the kind of look that his maths teacher used to give him when he couldn't grasp how a half multiplied by a half was a quarter.

"If you knew anything about hypnotism at all, you'd know that she first has to address the root cause of my addiction –she intends

52

to explore my childhood by regressing me, so that she can pinpoint the time I had my first fag. Then she'll probe me as to why I felt tempted and so on. After a bit of exploratory work, she's going to plant little triggers in my mind, so that whenever I see a Benson and Hedges King Sized, I'll associate it with something unpleasant and be repulsed by it."

David shook his head and smiled a sad, condescending smile. As a non-smoker, he could never understand what was to be gained by sucking on a cigarette and filling his lungs with toxic fumes.

"When I see a fag, I always associate it with something unpleasant automatically. I don't need a fifty-quid-an-hour hypnotist to tell me that. It's easy for me to criticize I suppose, not having an addictive personality."

Laz agreed. He was in half a mind to mention that David had swallowed eight cups of tea every day of his life since the age of four, but magnanimously let it pass. He wanted to get onto the main topic of the day, which was, of course, David's visit to London. He invited his friend to fill him in, omitting no detail, however slight. David pulled his chair closer and gave him the low-down, putting it across with much gusto and Italian-style arm-waving. Laz listened, rapt throughout; his mouth wide open in the style perfected and made its own by the halibut.

"You're in deep shit!" he concluded, once David had given his all. "Trilby is bound to quiz the National Gallery about you, which means, ipso bloody facto, that he'll discover that you are not just a complete nutter who has fabricated the whole thing, but someone who really *is* a top art restorer and who really *has* worked on a Van Gogh or two, but for some reason best known to himself, fabricated all the other stuff about gangs of art thieves and art restorers with made-up names. Not a complete nutter, in other words, but a partial nutter, if you follow me. When the gallery hears about your behaviour, it won't surprise me if they show you the door. You've become a security risk, and they're bound to think you're losing your marbles."

"Cheers!"

"Well, I have to tell it like it is, old pal. This bent copper could ruin you. You need to somehow get your retaliation in first. Can't you expose him as the Ashes thief or something?"

"How the bloody hell can I do that?" asked David hysterically, biting his nails and twitching like Herbert Lom used to do whenever he met Inspector Clouseau. "Inform the Daily bloody Mail that the Chief Superintendent of the Metropolitan Police intends to steal our greatest sporting treasure from under our noses? I wouldn't be just a partial nutter then - oh no! I'd be the full Monty. Secure unit job - strait-jacket - no sharp items. Especially if I explained that I'd based my theories on a conversation overheard between two drunken Aussies in a lavvie. Laz, let's face it. I'm in the shit, good and proper."

* * *

It would have been of some, albeit limited, consolation to the highly-strung overwrought artist, had he returned to Michael J. Trilby's office seconds after he had vacated it, cunningly disguised as a fly on the wall. He would have observed a nonplussed Chief Super pacing the floor and scratching his head, trying to articulate his feelings, which were many and varied.

The man he had just interviewed had got off to a bad start. He'd wandered in, seemingly full of confidence, but then suddenly wilted - his previously alert expression exchanged for one of distraction and panic. After appearing to be on the verge of collapse, he had rallied around and begun to babble about phallic symbols, felt pens and old masters, all so far-fetched as to be laughable. The man was clearly certifiable, but after many years in the force, Michael Trilby had learnt that truth was often stranger than fiction. There was no way that he was going to pester the National Gallery - not yet at any rate, but it would do no harm to put out a few feelers. Like all good nutcases, the man had omitted to leave his details, in spite of being asked to, but during his initial phone call he had apparently mentioned that he came from the Stourbridge area, which was a few miles away from Birmingham. Chief Superintendent Trilby knew the top man there, and it was the work of an instant to lift the bat-phone and have a word.

* * *

Laz could see that his friend was getting himself into a state. He toyed with the idea of a quick slap to the face, but shelved it, knowing full well that this would only make David even more hysterical. Instead, he tried to change the subject, and speak of lighter and more pleasant things. To this end, he enquired of the other's cricket session, and this seemed to do the trick. David had been doing some bowling, and was delighted and encouraged when one of his attempts had actually entered the nets and found its way to the batsman. His batting, too, had improved, in that he was connecting with the odd ball here and there and defending his wicket better. All positive stuff, considering that only a week previously he had swiftly deserted his crease every time the club's fastest bowler tossed one at him, a course of action that would have seen him shot at dawn before society became cognizant of such things as shell shock (or post traumatic stress disorder as it is now known). Barry Suggs was delighted with the improvement, but warned David that his maiden fifty was still a long way off.

Sensing that he had calmed down a little, Laz enquired of David as to the current state of the vandalized Van Gogh, and whilst his friend didn't exactly sink into the slough of despond or begin to hack at his wrists with a penknife, Laz could tell that he had taken him back to a place where he didn't wish to be.

"I haven't even started on it yet," sighed David. "It shouldn't take too long though. It's all about careful application of the right solvent with cotton buds, and hoping and praying that you don't dissolve the oil paint underneath in the process. I'll start on it later, if my nerves will stand it."

"And what if you do have to retouch the paint?" asked Laz. "How do you know what was underneath?"

"The gallery always sends a top quality photograph of the painting, which is true to the colour of the original, and an additional close-up showing the area affected, pre-graffiti, of course. That way we can reproduce the damaged area, if we need to. That's a last resort though. Hopefully the cleaning fluid will do the trick. Give me a lift home and I can show you if you like. Suzanne dropped me off this morning and I was going to walk back, but I need some company. If I'm on my own too much today, I might reach for the paracetamol bottle."

He threw his cricket kit into the back of Laz's car, and a short while later they were rolling onto the gravel drive of David's barn, where a police car awaited them. David gave his friend a look that spoke volumes, followed by a gulp that could be heard in the next county. Steeling himself for the inevitable, he took a deep breath and opened the car door. He had always been advised to approach the police car, rather than wait for the policemen to come to him. Apparently, they appreciated the polite gesture. With legs that seemed all of a sudden to be constructed of jelly, he staggered over to the Panda car with a gait that suggested that he'd been at the cooking sherry, and gently tapped on the driver's window. The window rolled down to reveal a face that he knew all too well.

"Ah! David. Long time no see. Say hello to David, Reg."

"Hello David!" said the passenger. "What have we been up to this time then?"

David emitted his trademark sigh and gazed heavenwards.

"Just when I thought life couldn't get any worse, it just did. Donald and Reg, how are you?"

"Excellent Dave, and who's the chap who looks like an extra in a pirate film?"

"Ah yes, this is my best mate, Laz. You've come close to meeting him on several occasions, believe it or not. Laz, this is Donald and Reg. Say hello to the lovely officers."

"Er, hello, lovely officers."

"Nice car, Laz," smiled Donald. "Yours, is it?"

"We might as well all come in for a nice cup of tea," said David resignedly. "Follow me up the steps."

Once inside the Fortress of Solitude, Reg made a bee-line for the comfy settee, which he proceeded to make his own by the clever arrangement of his long legs. Donald removed his cap and bagged the armchair, leaving Laz the hard wooden affair that was spattered with paint, and David standing.

"Nice to see you again," began Donald brightly. He was the vocal one of the pair, whilst Reg preferred the role of the Strong Silent Type. "I must say, you've filled out a bit round the middle since we last met."

"And his hair's going thin," added Laz helpfully.

David gave him one of his looks. "Yes, I have, haven't I? You pair, on the other hand, haven't changed a bit, but then again, you both looked about fifty when you were twenty-five."

"Dave..." said Laz.

"Don't worry, Laz," said David with a half-smile. "We've known each other for, how long is it, Reg? Twenty years. How come you're both still pounding the beat, lads? No promotions on offer? I thought your lot liked to reward mediocrity and incompetence."

"Dave..."

"Don't worry, Laz. The boys and I love a bit of light-hearted banter, don't we? You've probably heard me talk about Don and

57

Reg before. Remember when we were in our first band and George gave me that Gretsch guitar to look at after our first rehearsal? He thought maybe I could fix the electrics if you recall. Well it was Donald and Reg here who arrested me that night for suspected theft, and then let me walk four miles home in torrential rain, which ruined the guitar completely. The next time we met was when I was at Art College in Wolverhampton. That time they decided to perform a controlled explosion on my Mini Clubman, on the day I bought it. Meanwhile, the real buff-coloured Mini with the IRA explosives on board blew up half of the High Street."

Donald was looking slightly uncomfortable now, while Reg was just staring out of the window.

"Dave…" said Laz once more, his arm held high as if trying to attract the teacher's attention. David gestured for him to be silent and proceeded.

"And who can forget when they were called to Twopenny Green Aerodrome to catch the armed art dealer that I'd ensnared, and arrived half an hour too late? Maybe you will also recall the time when I mistakenly grabbed that police-woman from behind and thrust a banana into the small of her back, believing her to be an old friend of mine. It was Donald and Reg who were first on the scene on that occasion too, though I must admit that I did rather bring that one upon myself. The lads also arrested me for stealing a caravan the year after, even though I'd actually stolen it from the thieves who stole it from us. Are you seeing a pattern forming here, Laz?"

Laz buried his face in his hands and groaned.

"Shall we have a nice cup of tea?" suggested Reg tactfully.

David filled the kettle. "So what have I done this time, lads, as if I didn't know?"

"Well," began Donald, seemingly impervious to all the slings and arrows that David had slung at him. "We were having a nice cup of tea at base camp, minding our own business, when the boss pops his head around the door and enquires if any of us know of a 'care in the community patient' called David Day – his words, not ours - who professed to be an art restorer. Apparently the Chief Super from the Met had had this visitation from a Grade 'A' nutter – our words, not his – who was ranting on about international art thieves and black penises. Well, I took one look at Reg, didn't I Reg? And we said we'd look into it, so here we are. Over to you."

David poured the tea and took a new packet of HobNobs from his cupboard. He handed out mugs to his guests, perched himself on his draughtsman chair, took a very deep breath and began, ignoring Laz's attempt to interject.

"Look lads," he began wearily, "we've known each other for a very long time, and in that time I've got myself embroiled in a few hairy scrapes, have I not?"

"What does embroiled mean?" asked Reg, helping himself to two HobNobs.

"But think about it, lads. Have I ever been on the wrong side of the law, once the tale has fully unfolded? Didn't I always come out of the shit smelling of roses, blameless and without a stain on my character? Did you not end up collaring some prize villains, thanks to me? Come on, be fair."

Donald looked over at Reg, who looked back at Donald and nodded.

"He ith right," he spluttered through a mouthful of biscuit, sending debris all over David's freshly polished work surfaces. "You have to hand it to him, Don. We'd never have caught Lord Hickman or that dodgy Head of Department at his art college without Dave."

Donald weighed this and allowed David to continue.

"Lads, I'm in a bit of bother, I have to admit. I did go down to London to see the Chief Super about something of national importance, but something happened in his office, which prevented me from telling him the truth. I ended up having to concoct a complete load of lies; otherwise he'd have thought I was a nutcase."

"Well that didn't go to plan for a start," said Donald cheerfully. "So there's no Black Penis Art gang then? As if there could have been."

"No. And they aren't targeting the art restorers who are hired to remove the black penises either. It was all bollocks, I'm afraid."

"I see. No penis, but all bollocks. Pass me a HobNob, Reg, please. So why can't you tell us what you'd really gone to see him about? Don't you trust us?"

"Well, the straight answer to that is no, of course, but it's far more complex than that, Donald. It's, well, delicate, given that you two are coppers, and he's a copper..."

"Dave..." implored Laz, "could I..."

"In a second, Laz," said David impatiently. "Lads, if I told you something in the strictest confidence, would you promise to keep it quiet for a couple of days?"

"He just wants forty-eight hours," added Reg, with a faux American accent and more than a touch of sarcasm.

Donald was prevented from answering by the sudden and dramatic arrival of Suzanne. She flung the studio door open and burst in, dragging a small girl in a leotard behind her.

"Oh, there you are!" she exclaimed, her face all flushed and flustered-looking. "I see you've called them already. I'm so sorry. I don't know what to say. Oh my God!"

"What on earth is the matter?" asked David, the picture of concern.

"My Rolex is gone!" she wailed, "And I've only had it a week."

Donald chivalrously allowed her to sit down and invited her to explain.

"I only popped out to fetch Lauren back from her gymnastics, and when I got back, it was gone. I'd left it on the kitchen table while I cleaned your studio yesterday, when you went to London. I didn't want to scratch it you see. Well, I forgot to put it on this morning, and I've just gone to do so and it's disappeared."

"Was the kitchen door left open, Miss?" asked Donald.

"I'm afraid so. I was only gone ten minutes."

"Dave..." said Laz.

"You left the bloody house open?" asked David. "Are you barmy, woman? That watch cost two thousand quid!"

"Dave..." said Laz.

"Not now," said David tetchily.

"Dave," said Laz, a little more forcefully this time. "Where's your Van Gogh gone?"

Chapter 8

"Aargh! It's Tim!"

David was distraught and inconsolable in the order named, so Suzanne made tea whilst the officers busied themselves making copious notes. David paced the room, tearing out chunks of hair that he could ill afford to waste, and turned the air blue with profanities that thankfully meant nothing to Lauren, sat at the drawing board colouring in her picture book.

"And *you* went on to *me* about locking the house," said Suzanne, running her hands through her long, wavy hair in a distracted way. It's some bloody good building the Fortress of Solitude if you can't be bothered to lock it!"

"I was excited about going to cricket," David replied feebly. I popped in to try and work out the best way of removing the felt-pen penis first thing this morning, and I just forgot to lock up after me. I'm only human."

"Hang on," frowned Donald. "What do you mean, remove the felt-pen penis? You just told me that that was all a complete pack of lies. There was no Black Penis Gang, you said. Now you've changed your story again. I think it's time you came straight with us, don't you?"

Reg would have had something to say about it too, were it not for the fact that he was fast asleep on the settee. Donald explained that his partner would often do this after a whole packet of HobNobs. His condition was similar to narcolepsy, apparently, but it only came on after he'd gorged himself with food.

"That's what I was trying to explain, before Suzanne burst in," said David wearily. He desperately needed to slump into a chair, but Reg had commandeered three spaces all for himself.

"There *is* a real Van Gogh, and I *was* supposed to be restoring it, and it *did* have a felt-tipped penis on it."

"The penis had a felt-tip?"

"No. Shut up and listen. That much was true. The bit about international gangs that target restorers wasn't."

"Yeah! I can see that," said Donald, totally confused. "Were you insured, by the way?"

"Ah!" groaned David, "Good question. The thing is…"

"You weren't. My God! It's getting worse by the second."

"I was to start with, of course, but the premiums were getting prohibitive, and we just couldn't afford it, and it just sort of lapsed last year, didn't it, Suzanne?"

Suzanne didn't reply. She just stared out of the window, biting her lip.

"What's the matter, Daddy?" asked Lauren.

"Oh, Daddy's lost a painting, that's all. Don't worry about it."

"I'll draw you another one then," she said sweetly, and carried on colouring.

"Thanks mate," said David, gently stroking her hair, "Maybe I can offer it to the National Gallery when it's finished and then they won't mind losing their multi-million pound Van Gogh."

Donald decided that it was time to head back to the station, and began to gently rouse Reg, who was now snoring so loudly that it was becoming embarrassing.

"Look," begged David, "please, just for me, sit on this for a few days. There's something I can't tell you just yet, but if it comes off, there'll be big scalps on offer for you pair. It wouldn't surprise me if they made you Inspectors or something."

Donald hauled his bewildered-looking colleague unsteadily back onto his feet and they headed for the door. He turned and looked David square-on.

"Okay," he said, "here's the deal. We've witnessed a crime here, so it's our duty to investigate it. There's been a break-in, and a Rolex has been stolen. Regarding the figment-of–your-imagination Van Gogh that's been stolen by the imaginary gang of international art thieves, I'll ignore that for a bit, until such time you decide whether you've invented it all or not. As to the Chief Super, we'll try and pacify him somehow and get him off your back, but we need to be put in the loop as soon as possible, and if anyone needs collaring for anything, remember that you promised us first refusal, understand?"

"Agreed," replied David. He couldn't wait to break it to them about whom they were likely to be arresting.

Reg grabbed the one remaining HobNob, bade them farewell as if nothing untoward had occurred, and clumped down the studio steps with the other half of the Police Force's premier comedy duo. Laz watched intently as the Panda car rolled out through the gates, and then turned to address David.

"Right, you pair are in no fit state to do any rational thinking, so I'm taking charge. Here's my plan. Firstly, when is the National Gallery expecting this painting back?"

"Next Friday-ish," replied David brokenly.

"Okay. And what happens if you don't return it by then?"

"I'm dead."

"Okay. We know where we stand. What are the chances of recovering the painting before then?"

"Nil."

"Good. Then you must forge it."

"WHAT?"

"Forge it. Lauren gave me the idea just a while ago, bless her. You need breathing space. You told me that the gallery supplies top quality photographic reproductions of the picture, with sizes and so on. You're a master forger, so forge it."

"That's impossible!" said David. "Firstly, it has to be done on an aged canvas. The frame has to be exactly the same. If I painted it in oils, they wouldn't even be dry by Friday. Then I'd have to make it look a bit weathered - crack the varnish and so on. You don't know what you're asking."

"What's the alternative then?"

"There isn't one, unless you count putting my fingers into that light socket over there while I stand in a bucket of water."

"So you forge it. Start after lunch, is my advice."

David paced up and down his Fortress of Solitude, as Hamlet was prone to do when things got on top of him. Had his family and best friend not been present, he'd have probably sat on his pedal bin and off-loaded a lengthy soliloquy too.

"I could use an accelerant with the paint, to dry it out," he mumbled.

"Good. An accelerant is good," agreed Laz, the poor man's Horatio.

"I've got loads of old, period canvases and stretchers," added David.

"See? It's getting brighter all the time," said Laz.

"The frame was very simple really. Martin the framer could reproduce that at a price, I suppose."

"Course he could. Good man that Martin, if expensive."

"What about my Rolex?" Suzanne piped up.

"I know a bloke on the market who knocks them out for twenty quid," replied Laz, "and *his* fakes aren't bad either, as long as you don't look too closely at the seconds' hand."

* * *

Laz came round after work on Wednesday with a nice surprise, having surmised that his beleaguered friend needed a bit of cheering up. He found David in slightly better spirits, largely due to the fact that his forged Van Gogh was coming on a treat. The original painting was a very small example of the artist's work, and therefore relatively easy to reproduce, which helped a lot. Vincent himself would have completed it in one, maybe two sittings, which meant that a week was far more generous than had first been assumed. There was also good news from Martin the framer. He had managed to track down a frame moulding so similar to the one originally used that David merely needed to distress it a little and the job was done.

"What are you doing next week?" asked Laz, waving a white envelope around provocatively in front of David's eyes.

"Booking into a rest home for nervous artists in Cheltenham," he replied. "They put you in a wheel chair with a tartan shawl over you and this nurse pushes you around the tranquil, manicured gardens, occasionally wiping the drool from the corner of your mouth."

"Oh! So you can't come to Old Trafford then? I've got two tickets for the first test."

For the first time in what seemed ages, David raised a proper smile. He'd never been to a test match, and he was excited.

"That's brilliant, Laz. Count me in, as long as I'm not festering in a jail by then, of course, for faking an important work of art." He stopped work and cleaned his hog's-hair brush. "You know, this is all very weird. I can understand the Rolex. An opportunist thief watching the house, seeing Suzanne drive off and seizing his moment, but to come up here and target this specific painting - it's got to be an inside job. A layman wouldn't have even known what the picture was – I'm sure of it. It wasn't even very Van Gogh-like was it? It's one of his early works you see, and not typical to my mind. Maybe there is a Black Penis Gang after all, and I didn't just invent it. Maybe I'm going slowly insane, unable to differentiate between fact and fiction."

Laz fingered his chin, Holmes-like. "It could be someone at the gallery, feeding the information to the criminals, or it could even be the courier firm. No offence, but has Suzanne mentioned it to anyone? You know what women are like for gossiping."

"She wouldn't dare, Laz. I tell you, it's a mystery, but whoever took it, it'll be in the collection of some reclusive millionaire now, in a bank vault. We'll never see that again. I just hope they take care in removing the felt-pen todger."

"You never know, the thieves might think Van Gogh intended it to be there and leave it on," suggested Laz. "Can you imagine them trying to flog it to someone in the local pub? 'This is an early piece, from his Phallic Period, entitled 'Cock in a Cornfield.' It would take some selling in that condition, I reckon. Wouldn't it be worth a few phone-calls to small galleries, just to see if anyone had tried to fence it?"

"Forget it," said David, shaking his head. "It would be like looking for a needle in a haystack."

"Or a knob in a cornfield?"

"Exactly. I'm just hoping that the National Gallery simply

hangs this thing that I've painted back on the wall without examining it too closely. I don't suppose they'll be expecting their top restorer to fleece them, so they won't be looking for it. If I keep telling myself that, maybe I'll convince myself soon."

"I have every confidence in you, old pal," said Laz, massaging his friend's shoulder. "Here's your ticket – on me. We've got the opening day. I'll take you. Are you sure you're not tied up with deadlines?"

David perused his diary. "Oops! That was close. I've promised to teach at my old art college the day before. No, I'm fine! Just the antidote I need to all this stress."

* * *

Friday morning saw David looking even more tense than he had been all week. This was the day he wrapped the Van Gogh, assigned it to its flight case and waited for the doorbell to ring. It rang just as he was sipping his tea, which resulted in him wearing most of it. He nervously answered the door, eyeing the poor couriers with suspicion. He signed the necessary paperwork with shaking hand and said goodbye to his forgery, saying a silent prayer to his maker as he did so. That weekend saw him fretful and agitated; a condition made worse by the fact that no one from the gallery rang him back. In fairness, they never did, unless there was a problem, so no news was good news. Either that or it was very bad news. It was hard to tell.

He filled his time by training in the nets at Enville and taking Lauren to the park. It helped, but his mind was elsewhere. Sunday night he prowled the living room like a caged tiger, and left half of his dinner, which was unusual, because he loved Spaghetti Bolognese.

* * *

The following morning, David arrived at Wolverhampton College of Art, where he was to teach the foundation year students and set them an illustration project. It was a useful distraction, and meant that he'd be out of the studio all day, away from any National Gallery phone calls or police harassment. It was also a very poignant visit for him, as he'd spent his happiest years there, and was looking forward to renewing acquaintance with his old head of department, John Auberton.

John, a gentle-natured Welshman with a huge, toothy grin, was sitting in his cramped office poring over a pile of tedious paperwork when David tapped on the door and entered. The two men hugged each other and then John held David at arm's length. He didn't quite say, "Gosh! Let me look at you, my long-lost child!" but it was a close-run thing.

"It's weird," said David, once the preliminary exchanges were concluded, "how I'm sat here now, about to teach these students, when it only seems like yesterday I was here myself, being moaned at by you for leaving my holiday project in my old Mini that the police blew up. How come I look a million years older but you look exactly the same?"

"It's the teaching profession, Dave," grinned John, "we have such an easy, stress-free life, with such short hours and so many holidays, that it preserves our looks. And did you know that teachers never die in term time? Incredible but true. Did you ever hear of it happening, because I never have? It's only when our routine is buggered up by holidays, we lose our *raison d'etrê* and keel over. That's why I choose to be here all hours of the day. I hate it but it keeps me alive. Anyway, it's great to see you looking so healthy. You've even filled out a bit, but it suits you – you were like a bloody stick insect when you were here, man."

"Don't *you* start," laughed David, trying to suck his stomach in.

69

"So are this current crop of kids as good as we were? Truth now!"

A wistful, faraway look came into John's eye. "You'll think this is flattery, David, but you lot were a special year. You, Katie Black, Dylan Weldon – I've still got some of your stuff in my plan chest over there. Do you remember that series of drawings you did, called 'Patrick turns into a teapot'?

"My God! Have you still got those?"

John stepped over to the chest and pulled open the bottom drawer.

"Here you are, and there's Dylan's self-portrait. Remember that?"

David laid the drawings out on John's table and stared at them. Suddenly, and rather embarrassingly, a tear formed in David's eye. The slightly naïve, long-lost drawings seemed to have triggered something deep in his mind, releasing a flood of long-ignored bitter-sweet memories. He was unashamedly sentimental, but he sometimes wished he could persuade his emotions to wait until he was alone before they turned him into a gibbering wreck.

"Don't worry, David," whispered John kindly, "I'm the same."

David wiped his eyes on the sleeve of his coat. "It suddenly hit me that my life is hurtling along like a train, and heading for a destination I don't want to reach. Seeing these pictures brought it all back. Me and Dyl in the old café downstairs, scraping the money together for a Twix and two teas. Bob with his awful cowboy shirts. That dumpy little life-model with the unfeasibly massive boobs. All those mad nights at the Molineux Pub. That was twenty years ago, John. Life was so much fun and we were so innocent and carefree. Now it's full of stress and worry."

"It might be for you," smiled John. "I'm okay, boyo. I'm still here!"

David tried to pull himself together. He was in danger of

becoming seriously maudlin.

"So are there any students to get excited about nowadays?"

"Not really, I'm afraid. Art is a dying art, if this lot are anything to go by. Mainly dead-heads and no-hopers – a couple with a modicum of talent. They've got the right hair-dos and they look the part, but most of them are playing at it, and I can't see them ever getting a job at the end of it all, unlike you lot. I've asked you here today to see if you can impress them and fire them up a bit. I'm just that old git from Cardiff who moans at them, but you're the nearest thing we have to a celebrity - someone who works at the sharp end. They'll be impressed by what you've achieved, and hopefully it'll rub off on them. Some are already beyond redemption mind you. Leonardo himself could talk to them and it wouldn't affect them, that's presuming they even know who he was. The worst one is a chap called Tim. My advice is give up on him before you start. It saves time. He is utterly talentless, and accident prone."

"A bit harsh, perhaps?"

"Oh no. Remember Jonah, from the Dandy – or was it the Beano? Anyway, he'd board a ship and seconds later, it would sink. That's Tim. Tim rhymes with Dim. That's not just accidental. God planned it that way to warn us. Tim asked to use the darkroom yesterday. He'd been in there about three minutes and he set it on fire. I couldn't do that if I tried. He's been drawing a picture of Gary Glitter now for two terms."

"Nice choice."

"Exactly. It's easier to just let him carry on. It keeps him quiet. I keep going to go up to him and offer advice, but there's so much he doesn't know, I go all hopeless and give up; awful for a teacher to admit, but it's true. And now I've filled you with enthusiasm, let's go meet them, eh?"

He stood up, emptied his tea cup into the small, paint-stained sink and invited David to do likewise. Then, taking a fortifying deep breath, he led the way.

David spent the morning dispensing his pearls of wisdom, but it was mainly pearls before swine. He took a disproportionately long time attempting to show a stunningly attractive dark-skinned girl how to improve her 'mixed peppers' still-life group, before reluctantly heading for Tim Beasley.

Tim was sat at the far corner of the studio, studying Gary Glitter's eyes. One of them, he felt, seemed to be out of kilter with the other one, but he was blowed if he could decide which one was wandering off. It would need to be corrected, to prevent the pop star looking as if he had been tapped in the testicles with a mallet (though some would argue that this was what he was crying out for). David approached the desk and offered his two-pennyworth.

"Little Richard wasn't cross-eyed, Tim, as far as I'm aware."

"Erm, it's supposed to be Gary Glitter, sir."

"Call me David, please. Gary Glitter eh? It's more serious than I thought, in that case. You might need to do a little rubbing out, here and there. Don't be scared to start correcting stuff if it's not right. You've got to bite the bullet."

"I know."

"Be bold."

"I'm not good at that. I've been on this now for two terms, so I didn't really want to start rubbing it all out again, sir, David."

"Do you know how long this would have taken me to draw, Tim?"

"No, sir."

"About four and a half hours."

"Oh! Well I suppose you kind of speed up when you're a professional. I fink my problem is that I can't make artistic decisions. That's what Mr Auberton says. I've got this freelance job on at home; the first one I've ever been given, and I keep pondering over it."

"The strong hue of resolution is sicklied o'er by the pale cast of thought, eh?"

"Er, no. It's just that I get a good idea, but then I fink about it a bit, and then I'm not so sure."

"So what's this freelance job entail? I hope the client isn't desperate for it."

"He is. That's the problem. He's pressurizing me."

"Maybe he's middle-aged, and wants to see his portrait finished before he dies."

"No, sir, I'm not doin' a portrait. It's a bit of retouchin' that he wants doin', and I'm not sure how to proceed. He's got a nasty blemish on a paintin' of his, and he wants me to remove it."

David pulled up a chair. "You interest me strangely, Mr Beasley. What sort of blemish? Ketchup? Pigeon shit? Do tell!"

"I'd rarver not, sir."

"Bloody hell. It's not seminal fluid, surely? I get worked up about pictures – especially Vermeer, but …"

"It's graffiti. Somebody scribbled on it when they broke into his flat, and it's upset him, 'cause it was a present from his dead mother."

"Oh, I am sorry. Did she buy it for him after she'd died or before?"

"Before, I fink, and it's deeply sentimental to him."

David confided in Tim that he had recently been given a very

73

similar problem to solve, but in his case, the graffiti had been in the form of a crudely-drawn rendition of the male genitalia.

"Oh, right!" whispered Tim. "Well the graffiti on mine is a bit different to that." He glanced around the room to make sure no-one was eavesdropping. "It's a badly drawn willy."

David did a double-take that Laurel and Hardy would have been proud of.

"Repeat what you just said."

"It's a man's - you know - todger, sir."

David's eyes were like saucers now. "This painting. It wouldn't be of a cornfield would it?"

"Yes! How did you know that? Mr Auberton said you was good, but bloomin' hell, that was brilliant! It's a bit rough really, this picture, but the bloke likes it because he said it reminds him of his mother. He can't bear to look at it now though, wiv a knob on it, so he's paying me fifty quid to get it off."

"Fifty quid, eh?" said David, trying his hardest to keep a lid on his emotions. "That's a lot to a student. What were you going to use to remove the graffiti then?"

"I fort of using a bit of Jif and a scouring pad first, and then I planned to put the missing paint back in wiv some oil paints I had wiv the Paint by Numbers me muvver got me for Christmas."

David actually felt the blood migrate south from his face. He had to clutch onto the corner of Tim's desk to prevent himself from keeling over.

"Not wise," he croaked. "Tell you what. How would you like to *really* impress this bloke? Let me restore it for you, free of charge. How's that? You do realize I'm one of the best restorers in the country don't you?"

"Of course!" grinned Tim. "But why would you want to do that for me? Nobody else at this college ever gave a shit, sorry sir, a damn, about me."

"It's because I've seen a latent talent in you, Tim. I have faith in you, and I'll tell you what, when Gary Glitter is finished, I'll buy it off you - fifty quid cash."

Tim was ecstatic. He sensed a turning point in his so-far disappointing artistic career.

"Give me your address and I'll pick up the picture tonight. Better still, what are you doing lunchtime? I'll pay you up-front for Gary, so as you don't sell him to anyone else. I know just the place to put that. You needn't even correct his eyes. The more I look at him, the more I realize how perfect they are."

Aware that he was rambling, David shut up. He left Tim to his duties and decided to revisit the pretty, dark-haired girl to see how her peppers were developing.

At lunchtime, John wandered into the studio to rescue David and take him off to the pub for a quick pasty and a bit of reminiscing. Reluctantly, his old star pupil cried off, citing a prior engagement, but promised to join him for a tea break during the afternoon session. He met Tim in the staff car park and invited him to jump into his Mercedes, offering a silent prayer as he did so. If John was right about Tim being a Jonah who could raze a darkroom to the ground in seconds, what could he do with a thirty-thousand pound car full of petrol? The Mercedes sped off in the direction of Pensnett, where Tim lived, its driver's eyes nervously alternating between the road and his passenger.

Tim was mightily impressed with David's car, and insisted on asking what all the various gadgets did, only to find each polite request met with the same, terse, "Don't touch it!"

Bathed in sweat, David eventually fetched up at Tim's parents' modest semi. His passenger dashed inside and emerged seconds later with the painting in a plastic Spar bag. David grabbed it and removed the picture. Glory be! It was unscathed, if one discounted the large black member standing proudly erect in the cornfield.

"Thank you, thank you, thank you!" smiled David. "Here's your fifty quid."

"And here's Gary!" replied Tim, opening his portfolio and proudly handing over his dog-eared, cross-eyed creation, still nonplussed as to why his eminent new friend was so excited about the prospect of erasing a felt-pen doodle.

"When can I have it back?" he asked. "Only this bloke wanted it in a hurry."

"I bet he did. I'll need four days minimum. Tell him he'll have to wait. You can't rush a perfectionist. He should know that if he saw any of your work. I'll drop it round here for you Friday afternoon, so you can arrange to meet the man any time after that. And can I give you some professional advice?"

"Of course, David, sir."

"When he picks it up, get this bloke to sign something to say he's received it and he's happy with the job. Get his address and phone number as well. You mustn't forget that. We professional artists - and I include you here - *always* remember to do that. It's what we call a, erm, database. You'll also need it as, erm, evidence in case the taxman comes calling. Do you understand?"

Tim nodded earnestly. Name, address and phone number. He could do that. He was a pro now. That's what pros always did.

David started the engine and reversed out of Tim's cul-de-sac, feeling truly happy for the first time in a couple of weeks. At last he was turning a corner, and not just literally.

Tim, meanwhile, was glowing. He'd been helped out of a spot by a top professional, whom he now counted as a friend, and he'd also sold his first picture. Life didn't get much better. He would walk into college for the afternoon session with a swagger.

"What happens if you shove this button in, Dave?" he asked, as he made himself a touch too comfortable in David's cream leather passenger seat.

David glanced down at the cigar-lighter and offered another quick prayer.

Chapter 9

An Inspector Calls

Donald was on the phone, and Reg could tell that it was someone of importance on the other end of the line, because Donald was pronouncing his aitches and standing to attention. He'd even ditched his fag.

"Yes, sir," he said, "I managed to track down your suspect by hemploying a few little techniques I've learnt over my many years in the force. I'm a good, old-fashioned copper, sir, and I keep my ear to the ground."

The Chief Super reminded Donald that brevity was the soul of wit.

"...so I paid this fellow a visit," continued the constable, unperturbed, "and I think I can confirm his story. You were concerned that Mr Day was, to use your expression, a fantasist, if I remember rightly, sir, and given the evidence, who could blame you? I can assure you that he really is what he told you he was – a well-known art restorer – and while we were at his studio we discovered that an original Van Gogh that he had been asked to restore had been purloined, along with his wife's Rolex. No sir, not Van Gogh's wife, I meant Mr Day's wife. Yes, sir. The missing painting had apparently been defaced with a crude drawing of a male member, but I can't confirm this, due to the fact that the picture had already been purloined by the time we got there. No sir, we can't prove that Mr Day ever really had a Van Gogh with a willy on it, I realize that, sir. That's a very good point. I would add at this convenient juncture though, sir, that, as it transpires, we have had dealings with this gentleman before, and though he seems to get into all sorts of odd scrapes, he is basically sound and law-abiding, and I would go as far as to say I would personally vouch for him, in that respect. Yes, sir. I daresay he has informed the gallery by now. Very good, sir. Goodbye!"

Donald replaced the receiver and gawped at his partner. "Bloody hell, Reg. The Big Chief from Scotland Yard, phoning me! I promised Dave I'd smooth things with the Super, which I've done, so I hope to God the bugger doesn't let us down.

* * *

Chief Superintendent Trilby replaced the receiver. He was no wiser now. In fact, he was a damned sight more confused. Call it an old copper's instinct, but he was totally convinced that the vague, nervous-looking man who had visited him the week before was making up his story as he went along. Michael Trilby prided himself on being an expert at interpreting body language, and David's spoke volumes. The man was either completely mad or trying his best to think on his feet – almost as if he'd been forced to change his script at the eleventh hour. Surely no one was really called Carrivan Innadich; it was preposterous. The man was clearly floundering. And yet, here was an experienced, if decidedly pedestrian constable from Stourbridge verifying his story. Or was he? Mr Day was indisputably a well-known art restorer, but that didn't prevent him from also being a fantasist. The man could have had a nervous breakdown, lost the plot, and begun to imagine that gangs were after him. Maybe years of restoring valuable paintings had made him paranoid and delusional. Didn't a lot of great artists go that way? One only had to look as far as Van Gogh himself to prove that theory. Then there was the evidence, or lack of it. What proof was there that the Van Gogh painting, with or without its penis, had ever existed? The constables arrived to find it and the Rolex gone. Anyone could play that game! We could all summon the cops to investigate our missing multi-million pound paintings, but the insurance bods liked to see a bit of proof – a photo maybe, or a receipt at least. No, the constable's investigations counted for nothing. They just proved that the man was an artist. Big deal! There was only one way to settle this, and that was to phone the National Gallery.

Michael Trilby buzzed his secretary and asked her to get him the curator, pronto. Seconds later, Henry Tibbatts was on the line.

"Good day, Mr Tibbatts – I'm sorry to bother you. It's a personal call, so don't be concerned unduly. I wonder, can I ask you about a Mr David Day? I think I'm right in saying that he occasionally works for you."

"Ah! David. He does indeed. Lovely man, head in the clouds more often than not, but one of our most gifted artists. What's the problem?"

"Oh, no problem whatsoever. I play the odd round of golf with him when he's in London. Smashing lad! I just wondered how good an artist he was, but you've already answered my question. My grandmother died recently and left me what has been described as a very expensive oil painting. The only trouble is, it's been damaged. She succumbed to dementia, you see, and attacked it one day with her umbrella, because she was convinced it was giving her a funny look. I was thinking of asking our David to repair it, once I've popped over to Australia for the last time to tie up a few things and ship it back."

The curator affected what is commonly known as the sharp intake of breath, as employed by plumbers when asked for an on-the-spot quote.

"David is your man, sir, but he ain't cheap. It depends on the value of this picture. Who is it by, may I ask?"

Chief Superintendent Trilby was panicking. "Erm, you have to excuse me, Mr Tibbatts, I'm useless at art, and I've forgotten. Could it be, erm, Sir Malcolm Sergeant?"

"I wouldn't have thought so. He was a conductor."

"Oh! What about Constable then?"

"Well, if it *is* a Constable, you've reduced the rank considerably, but vastly increased the price. Are you *sure* it's a Constable? They are very hard to come by nowadays."

"Yes, Constable rings a bell. I'm sure they said Constable. Does that mean I'm rich?"

"Oh yes, if it's kosher, and your grandmother's brolly hasn't buggered it. You said she thought it was looking at her? Is it a portrait then? Constable was mostly known for his landscapes."

Superintendent Trilby was getting out of his depth altogether now. "Oh really? No, it's not a portrait. Apparently, it's, erm, a farm labourer or peasant in a field having a rest, and his eyes follow you round the room. That's how you tell it's a good painting isn't it?"

"Er, no, actually, but never mind that. We wouldn't mind taking a look at it ourselves when you return from down under, and yes, ask David to quote you for restoring it, *if* we're talking a genuine Constable. He's just repaired a small Van Gogh for us, and I must say, it's a great job. It looks cleaner and brighter now, like a brand new painting!"

"Excellent! Is the picture back on show again? I wouldn't mind having a nose at it myself."

"Of course!" replied Mr Tibbatts. "As a matter of fact, I was looking at it just now."

Michael Trilby's frown deepened. "Well, I'm sorry to pester you over such a trivial thing. I must leave you to get on. Oh, one more thing. Have you ever heard of The Black Penis Group?"

"The *what?* No, sorry! I'm not up on all these new art movements I'm afraid. I'm a Renaissance man myself. Why?"

Michael Trilby assured him that it wasn't important, said his goodbyes and put the phone down. If he was confused before, it was nothing compared to what he was feeling now. He ran the gamut of emotions from A to Z, and then back to A again for good measure. Still he could make no sense of it all. Someone wasn't telling him the whole story, and Michael. J. Trilby was a man who liked to know the minutiae.

* * *

It had been a hell of a week in terms of variety and human achievement. On Wednesday, David had played the altruistic elder statesman of art, dispensing his vast knowledge to the spellbound students of Wolverhampton, knowing full well that his words of wisdom would enter their left ears and leave by their right ones, seconds after he had left the building. His reward for this hard day's slog was poor in monetary terms, but he had struck gold with Tim Beasley. Not only had David saved a major painting from Tim's Jif and Paint by Numbers butchery, he had potentially ensnared a thief in the process.

Thursday saw David and Laz in Manchester, enjoying a day at the test match, and what a day it was. England won the toss and elected to bowl, believing that the pitch would be problematic to the batsmen. The Old Trafford ground traditionally suited spin, so England chose two spinners, Phil Tufnell and a debutante named Peter Such. The Australians, on the other hand, preferring fast bowlers, only took along one spinner, a young man by the name of Shane Warne. In spite of Australia's opening batsmen knocking up a hundred before getting themselves out, all seemed to be going to plan, and shaping up to become a cracking game of cricket. It had been a wrench, having to leave at close of play. David and Laz had really enjoyed the change of routine, and for one wonderful day, all their troubles had seemed to melt away. Strangely, a physical reminder of their troubles manifested itself in the guise of two drunken Australian fans, as they made their way back to Laz's car. Mervin and Brett had drawn attention to themselves by jaywalking into the path of a Marks and Spencer's van, causing the driver to screech to a smoky halt and dislodge a few thousand chicken and mushroom pies. Having quickly assessed that the driver was approximately the size of two separate gorillas, with more tattoos than Lydia the Encyclopedia, they legged it at a rate of knots, giving both the driver and Laz the slip. A search of all the local hostelries produced nothing. The Aussies had vanished into the bush and gone walkabout.

Friday saw David back at the Fortress of Solitude, beavering away at his latest project, leaving his post only rarely for the occasional plate of sandwiches and mugs of strong coffee. It was not until Sunday morning that he finally emerged, bleary-eyed and exhausted to inform Suzanne that the task was completed. After a quick bacon and mushroom sandwich and a pot of tea, he returned to his studio to take another good, long look at the painting. He was pleased, if a little delirious, courtesy of some serious sleep deprivation. Copying a painting once is hard enough. Copying it twice was beginning to get past a joke. These Van Goghs were breeding faster than Dutch rabbits.

Having earlier managed to remove the graffiti with no bother whatsoever, he wrapped the original painting in brown paper and bubble wrap, and placed it in a sturdy box. That just left version number two at the National Gallery and version number three sitting on his easel. The accelerants in the paint would dry it out by the afternoon; just in time to hand it over to Tim. As long as old Jonah didn't put his foot through it or accidentally set it on fire, the picture would be in the hands of the mystery thief by

Sunday night, and providing Tim remembered to get the necessary information, it would only be a matter of time before the scoundrel was doing time and existing on gruel, weevils and stale bread. David's only regret was that his accomplice combined the brainpower of a moth with the physical grace of Mr Pastry, but there was nothing much that could be done about that. At least, if all else failed, Tim could describe the man to the police, and identify him in a line-up.

Even more taxing was the question of the original Van Gogh. David was by nature a very conscientious and law-abiding individual, as Donald had explained to his superior. The fact that he had conned the National Gallery was weighing heavily. He therefore needed to formulate a plan whereby the painting could be returned, unnoticed. He wracked his brains, but no solution came to him. There was no way he could boldly march into the gallery and quickly swap the pictures. Security would have his arm folded up his back in seconds, and steel shutters would be slamming down left, right and centre. Neither could he ask for the picture to be sent back to him in order that he could effect the switch at home. What possible artistic reason could he concoct for demanding its return? "I'm a perfectionist and I wasn't quite happy with it, Mr Tibbatts," didn't ring true, somehow.

David decided to confine the problem to the back burner for the time being, hoping that one of his famed inspirational flashes would come to him. Meanwhile, he resolved to bite the bullet and phone Tibbatts. He'd heard nothing from him since receiving the fake, so if he sounded happy, it would buy David more time to resolve the problem. He dialed the number with shaking hand.

"Henry, how are you?" he began, with only the slightest hint of a tremor in his voice. "Just having a lazy afternoon, so I thought I'd ask how the, erm, Van Gogh went down."

"A beautiful job as always, David," beamed Henry. David was so relieved that his legs buckled, and he had to sit down.

"I had your mate, the Chief Super on, not long ago," Henry continued.

David's new-found composure disappeared as quickly as it had arrived. "What?"

"The Chief Super, Mr Trilby. I didn't realize you were golfing partners."

"Neither did I."

"David, you're such a comedian, honestly. Is it a Black Country thing?"

"Must be. What did he want then?"

"He was asking about your artistic skills, but it's best he explains it himself when you next play a round together. Mind you, he's returning to Australia soon, so maybe you won't get a chance."

"Is he now? I wonder why."

"Oh, he's about to become the proud owner of a national treasure from what he was hinting. He could end up a rich man."

"Really?"

"Look, it's none of my business. It's best he explains things to you himself. Now if you'll excuse me, I must fly. There's a Renoir just arrived from France that I need to look at. Oh, and I recommended you to a friend the other day, by the way. Do tell me if it comes off. Graham Gunmore-Nicholls; you won't forget a name like that will you? Toodle-oo!"

If Chief Superintendent Trilby had seemed perplexed after his call to Henry Tibbatts, it was nothing to the effect that the curator's conversation had had on David. Had his studio been plagued with flies, most of them would have ended up in David's mouth. Golf partners? Bosom buddies? Here was a Chief Super who had been hitting the gin and tonics well before the sun had gone over the yard arm. He probably had one of those ornamental globes in his office full of the stuff, and the result was that his once-sharp copper's brain had turned to mush.

Or had it? The wily old devil was surely probing. He knew full well that Henry would relate their conversation to his favourite restorer. The bit about national treasure was especially interesting. Unless David was very much mistaken, the brazen and corrupt policeman was rubbing it in. Could Trilby be challenging him? Teasing him, knowing full-well there was nothing a mere artist could do to stop a powerful police chief. David would have to tread very carefully, and have eyes in his backside; it would be so easy for Trilby to get him bumped off. Maybe this was a warning – a subtle shot across the bows, unwittingly delivered by David's employer.

There was only one thing to do. David put the kettle on.

Chapter 10

Tim Beasley – Secret Agent

Turning into Tim Beasley's cul-de-sac, David parked outside his parent's house. Immediately, the curtains started twitching. It was one of those streets. Tim ran out from the front door and tripped up on a flagstone. He came a purler down the steps, losing his glasses in the neglected and un-mown grass, en-route to bashing his brow against the low picket fence. Miraculously, he sprang to his feet as if nothing had happened and proceeded, albeit a little unsteadily, to David's car.

"Lord help us!" whispered David as he reached over to open the passenger door, an action less to do with politeness than the desire not to have his door handle wrenched off. Tim threw himself inside, whacking his head on the rear-view mirror in the process.

"Worro David!" he beamed. "I can't wait to see this."

David smiled at him sweetly, and suppressing an overwhelming urge to crown him with a building brick, reached over for the carrier bag on the back seat.

"Here you are," he said, revealing his masterpiece. "Not a knob in sight!"

"It's like it was never there!" gushed his pupil. "You are a genius!"

"I know," said David. "Now please, carry it carefully, make sure your laces are tied, avoid uneven surfaces and all combustible substances. Go to your rendezvous and hand it over, claim your reward, of which I want no part, and please, please please, remember what I asked you to do, vis-à-vis the man's details. Study him like a hawk and remember his every facial detail. Understood?"

"Yes, sir, but I can't see why I need to do all that."

"Yours," explained David slowly, "is not to reason why. Yours is but to do or die. Is that clear, Gungadin?"

Tim nodded. These famous artists were very odd, he mused, but he was so grateful and in awe of his new mentor that he would have jumped off a cliff had David suggested it.

"I have a few things to do, Tim, so I'm going to have to leave you to it. Kid to bathe, dog to walk and so on. Ring me as soon as you can tonight, once the deed is done. Here's my home number. Once you have used it, eat it."

* * *

David was watching the cricket highlights on T.V. England seemed to have snatched defeat from the jaws of victory as usual, helped in no small part by the Australian spin bowler, Shane Warne. Mike Gatting, the England batsman, was renowned for his ability to play the spin bowlers, so when young Mr Warne was brought on, Gatting was probably glancing around at the crowd, acknowledging their cheers with a regal wave while thinking to himself that here was an easy double century in the making. He may even have nonchalantly flicked a spec of lint from his sleeve – he was that confident. Then young Shane took his tiny little five-step run up, if 'run' is the correct word for his casual little amble towards the wicket, and flicked a slow ball at Gatting that changed the entire nature of the test match, and cricket history, for that matter. The leg break floated down the pitch, gathering pace and drifting prodigiously to the leg side, eventually bouncing well outside Gatting's leg stump. Gatting responded by thrusting his leg towards the leg side and keeping his bat close to his pad to create a wide barrier against the unpredictable spin of the ball. Warne's ball, however, deviated from its pre-bounce trajectory by a truly astonishing amount, disappearing behind Gatting and clipping the top of his stumps.

Gatting just stood there, feeling perplexed, dumbfounded and nonplussed simultaneously. He was probably also vexed, miffed and irritated, not to mention embarrassed, belittled and devastated. Strangely though, his face just registered a simple look of confusion, and it seemed like an eternity before reality kicked in. Warne and the boys were whooping and hollering, and calling poor Mike Gatting playground names. Eventually, once he'd checked with the umpire that he hadn't just dreamt it all, he trudged his weary way back to the pavilion to have a lie down. Captain Graham Gooch, in the post-match press conference, said that portly old Mike Gatting looked like a man who had just had his lunch stolen. Meanwhile, cricket buffs around the world were calling Warne's opening gambit the ball of the century, and, painful though it was for an Englishman to watch, David was very pleased to have seen a little bit of history in the making before the phone rang. Ordinarily he would have been irritated by such an interruption, but he knew this wasn't some cretin trying to sell double-glazing. At least, he hoped it wasn't. He dashed to grab the receiver and locked himself in the kitchen, away from the noise of the T.V., thus giving Suzanne the perfect opportunity to switch channels.

"How'd it go?" he asked, forgetting to wade through the pleasantries first. After all, Agent Beasley was on the other end, and knowing him, the money would run out, or the kiosk would be demolished by a runaway truck before he got to the juicy bits.

"Transaction completed," whispered Agent Beasley. "The eagle has landed. Picture handed over wivout incident, well, more or less – I managed to lose my specs case down the loo when I bent over to flush the fing, but uvver than that, operation successful."

"Did he like it?"

"Fort it was fantastic!"

"Good. Paid you, did he?"

"Fifty notes."

"Excellent! Got his details?"

"Oops! I knew I'd forgot somefink."

"WHAT?"

"Only kiddin'. Got his details."

"How amusing. Read them to me, there's a love."

"Barry Suggs, nineteen, Newbery Terrace…"

"Say that again."

"Barry Suggs…"

"Thanks, Tim," said David, "I need to go. I'm being called. I was halfway through dinner and it's getting cold."

David returned to the living room where his cricket documentary had mysteriously metamorphosed into a programme about tortoises. It could have been a documentary about naked Swedish *au pairs* and he wouldn't have noticed. His mind was reeling. Barry Suggs was the fourth most unlikely person to have stolen things from his house, after Suzanne, Laz and his mother - the fifth if he included Bamber Gascoigne. Barry was the Enville cricket captain, for God's sake. Men like that didn't nick off with Van Goghs and Rolexes. It just wasn't…..well, cricket.

* * *

Saturday's cricket practice was a strange affair. Barry had waltzed over to David as soon as he arrived and offered him a place at number eleven in the third team for the following day, which was thrilling, if a little daunting. The team was playing at home against nearby Wombourne, who were eager to avenge a recent drubbing. As the two men spoke on the pavilion steps, David eyed Barry up and down, looking for signs that the man was a master criminal. He found none. He decided on plan B, which was to bring up the topic of burglary and see if anything registered in Barry's expression. He'd borrowed the idea from Hamlet, when the suspicious prince penned a play closely mirroring the King's suspected misdemeanours and made him sit through it, noting his reaction as the actors performed.

Upon hearing of David's break-in, Barry, it was fair to say, reacted very theatrically indeed. Something, it appeared, had got inside of him and was making him agitated, but it transpired that Barry was displaying the ire of the victim, and not the guilt of the criminal.

"Don't get me started on theft," he spat. "I've only just begun to calm down."

David invited him to sit down before he had a stroke, and probed him gently.

"I went out to the pub on Thursday to watch the test highlights, and when I got home, my beloved Kawasaki Ninja was gone."

David looked concerned. He'd have looked even more so had he known what a Kawasaki Ninja was.

"My motorbike," explained Barry, still clearly upset by it all. "I use it to go to work on, and now I'm having to catch the bus. All thieves should have their testicles removed with a cheese-wire, shortly before they are boiled in oil and tossed off a cliff for the sharks to eat."

91

"You disapprove of them?"

"Oh yes."

"I was picking up on that - reading between the lines, as it were. Do the police have any clues?"

"Not as yet, no, and neither do I. The weird thing is, the keys were taken from my house, and I keep them in a very unusual place. No one but my wife knows where I keep them, and that's a fact."

This story was ringing bells with David. Had he shared a small Bed and Breakfast with a campanologist's convention, the effect couldn't have been any more striking.

"My break-in was exactly the same," he said, drawing up his chair and glancing around to check that no one was eavesdropping. "You don't reckon our wives are in it together do you?"

Barry discounted this theory with a wave of the hand. "The current and final Mrs Suggs is a saintly woman. Dismiss that thought from your mind, and while you're feeling dismissive, dismiss any thoughts about the current and final Mrs Day too. Especially as the thief nicked her Rolex as well as one of your paintings."

David had told Barry half of the truth, omitting to mention that the painting was in fact worth several million pounds, which precluded it from being one of his own. He looked into his captain's eyes once more as they sat comparing notes. If this man was an accomplished art thief, David was a capybara in a tutu. Presuming David had got that much right, why on earth would the man in the pub choose Barry as his alter-ego? David excused himself to visit the lavatory, so that he could think things through.

As he sat in the cubicle – the same one he'd occupied whilst listening in on Mervin and Brett, for he was a creature of habit – David examined the facts.

A man had stolen a painting of incredible value from his house, and ignored all the other very stealable items that offered themselves; items that would have appeared to the casual observer to be far more valuable than the painting. Tim Beasley had not only been given Barry's name, but he had also described the man as looking like Barry. The thief then, by David's reckoning, should look a lot like Barry but not *be* Barry. So far this made sense. Maybe Barry had a brother or cousin who didn't like him very much. This might just about explain how he knew the whereabouts of the bike keys. It still didn't explain, however, how the thief came to know about the Van Gogh. It was possible that the miscreant was a member of the cricket club, but David couldn't remember bumping into anyone that vaguely resembled Barry Suggs. The problem was, if David casually asked if Barry had any friends or relatives that resembled him, Barry would naturally want to know why David had asked, and there wasn't an easy excuse at hand to cover that one.

Then there was the motorbike incident. It appeared that Barry was not only being set up as a thief, but being robbed at the same time. Someone out there didn't like the Enville captain very much, and David needed to know who. He concluded his business and wandered over to find Barry again.

"I've just been chewing this over," said David. "Is there someone who doesn't like you at this club?"

"Only those who've copped one in the box from one of my fast balls. Other than that, no, I hope!"

"Fair enough. Just a thought."

The conversation was interrupted at this point by an extremely irritating wasp, which seemed to think that constantly buzzing around David's head was in some way worthwhile and even amusing. David was terrified of wasps, and couldn't see what their purpose was. Spiders caught flies and slugs were there to give hedgehogs something to eat, but wasps were, he felt, not one of

God's creations, but almost certainly one of Lucifer's. He leapt out of his seat and began to flail around like a demented banshee. This was nothing, however, to the reaction that this little, striped Piranha of the insect world was provoking from Barry Suggs. In sharp contradistinction to David's wild gestures, Barry had become very pale and sweaty, and seemed to be hyperventilating.

Eventually, after David had introduced the creature to its maker, courtesy of the Daily Mail colour supplement, he turned to find that Barry had turned grey and was pumping out gallons of salty liquid from virtually every pore he possessed. Fearing he'd had a heart attack, David began to loosen the man's collar, but Barry, who was beginning to slowly regain his composure, waved him away.

"I'm sorry, David," he said breathlessly, "but it's a phobia. I've had it since I was eleven, when a swarm of them attacked me at my parents' caravan in Ludlow and I ended up in hospital. I'm petrified, I'm afraid. Very silly for the big, hard cricket captain I know, but I have no control over it. The trouble is, I'm always seeing them out in the field, and I just freeze. Last year, I had a turn just as this bloke bowled a fast one at me, and it just hit me full on in the head. I was more concerned about the wasp that was on my pads."

"No need to feel embarrassed," said David sympathetically. "I hate them too, but if it affects you that badly, couldn't you see someone about it? Laz is seeing Dick Nibbells's sister about his smoking. Couldn't you try that?"

"Ha!" replied Barry, "I am doing, as it happens. The trouble is, she reckons it takes at least twelve sessions for something like that and I've only been twice so far."

"Did I hear the Nibbells name taken in vain?" asked a passing Dick Nibbells.

"Oh, we were talking about phobias," explained David, grateful that Dick had interrupted them just before he'd had chance to add something deeply sarcastic about hypnotists to Barry's earlier comment. "Barry here hates wasps."

"Is that so?"

"Yes, wasps and motorcycle thieves."

Dick pulled up a chair. "You've had your bike nicked?"

"Yep!"

"I got home last night and my caravan was gone."

"I didn't know you had a caravan," said Barry.

"I haven't now," replied Dick.

Barry was about to probe further, but was interrupted by the arrival of Laz, who appeared to be incandescent with rage.

"What on earth's up with your fizzhog?" asked David, concerned.

Laz sank into a chair and released around twelve choice expletives into the atmosphere, before adding,. "Some shitbag has stolen my nine-eleven."

"WHAT?"

"My beloved Porsche. If I catch whoever did it, I'll rip their bloody arm off and thrash them with the wet end of it. I keep a spare key under Dennis Taylor in my front garden. Nobody, but nobody knows it's there, except Annie of course."

Barry didn't want to stop Laz mid-flow, but curiosity got the better of him.

"Dennis Taylor, the snooker player?"

"Yes."

"He's in your front garden?"

"It's a garden gnome, but Annie and I thought it looked just like

Dennis Taylor."

"Oh, right."

"It was just in case one of us lost our keys and we were desperate, you see."

Did the thief steal Dennis as well?" asked Barry.

"No."

"So we're looking for a thief with exquisite taste. So far, if it's the same bloke, he's had it away with a Rolex, an oil painting, a Kawasaki top-of-the-range bike, a caravan and a Porsche nine-eleven. We know he likes the high life and he's not a snooker fan."

"Funny!" groaned Laz, who clearly thought otherwise.

David glanced around him. The pavilion was filling up with people trying to watch the test highlights on the club's minuscule and temperamental television set, or waiting to play cricket themselves in the Enville league match that was about to commence. Spud and his friend Ryan strolled across the grass and paused to say hello. David enquired as to Ryan's mother, Pauline's health, following the ice cream tub incident.

"She's sort of okay," mumbled Ryan, "but she acts a bit weird now and again, like."

"What, she thinks she's Napoleon, you mean?" asked David.

"Nah!"

"She speaks in tongues?"

"Do what?"

"Any memory loss or delirium?"

"I dunno what you're on about."

David was beginning to realize that, whilst technically, he and most thirteen-year-olds spoke the some language, there was seldom a meeting of minds. He abandoned his enquiry on the grounds that there were more pressing matters to deal with and he didn't care that much in the first place.

"Wish her well for me then," he concluded, knowing full well that Ryan probably wouldn't remember to pass on his good wishes anyway.

Meanwhile, Dick had left the party to continue rolling the pitch, leaving Laz and Barry to fume on their own. Laz was extolling the virtues of public beheadings, while Baz preferred birching and national service, followed by hanging. Being realists, they realized that their policies had little chance of making it to the statute books, so in the meantime they'd had to make do with Donald and Reg of the Stourbridge police, whom they had both contacted earlier. David said nothing, but in his mind he could see a lop-sided old wooden sign, covered in cobwebs and bearing the legend, 'Abandon all hope, ye who enter here.'

Having commiserated with his fellow Victims of Theft Club members, David drove home, thankful that he still had transport. He opened the front door and looked over at the phone to see if he'd been left any messages. The red light was flashing, so he grabbed a notepad and pencil and pressed the button.

Message one. "Hello Ethel, where are you? You're normally at the bingo, so I wondered if you'd had another of your turns. It's me, Maureen."

*

Message two. "David. It's Chief Superintendent Trilby here. I think we probably need a little chat."

*

97

Message three. "Dave - Donald speaking. Why is it that you are always at the epicentre of things? I've had Larry Homer screaming blue murder because someone stole his Porsche, followed by another mate of yours, Barry Suggs, doing likewise about his Kawasaki. The Chief Super is convinced you are a fantasist because the painting you assured me was stolen is apparently safe and sound at the National Gallery, so where does that leave your wife's Rolex? Was that a pigment of your imagination as well? Me and Reg will pop in for a nice chat and a cup of tea soon. Bye!"

*

Message four. Oh hello! My name is Graham Gunmore-Nicholls. You were highly recommended by Henry Tibbatts at the National Gallery. We have a piece here that is in need of restoration. It is being sent by Securigard to reach you first thing Monday, and we hope you will be able to help us out. Henry assures me that your work is of the highest possible standard, and you are used to dealing with priceless works of art. I don't wish to mention the precise nature of the job over the phone, just in case, but I would be grateful if you could contact me on receipt and I will explain what needs doing. My number is …"

*

Message five. "Hello Dearest. Lauren and I are down at Merry Hill, and I've seen some nice trousers in the Debenhams' sale, so I'll get them for you. I noticed that your green ones are all frayed at the bottom. I'll be back late, so if you're hungry there's a frozen thingy in the freezer compartment. It's a bit out of date but it won't hurt you. My mother eats them when they're weeks over and she's alright. Bye!"

*

"Physically maybe," David mused, plumping for the safer cheese and lettuce sandwich option. As he stood preparing his lonely supper, he wondered if Henry would still have recommended him so highly to Mr Gunmore-Nicholls had he realized that there was a fake hanging where his Van Gogh used to be.

Chapter 11

A Surprise Package

David was feeling stiff. Sunday's game – his first real full-length affair, had gone quite well, considering his lack of skill and experience, but he was paying for it now. He was aching all over, and at seven-thirty a.m. that morning he feared Suzanne would have to snap his limbs in order to extricate him from their bed. Much to his delight and astonishment, he'd managed to take an easy catch and knock nine runs before getting bowled out. Enville had lost, but the damage was already done before he turned up at the crease, so he couldn't be held directly responsible. It was a tall order for the final two batsmen to manage one hundred and seventy-four runs, and, all things considered, it was a good start for him. He'd fully expected to be out for a duck, so nine was wonderful, but still a good way off the fifty he needed to produce before the end of the season.

Dragging himself up the studio steps one at a time, like an arthritic octogenarian, he finally reached the door and let himself in. The first ten minutes were spent slumped in the chesterfield, staring at the ceiling. If this was how he was to feel after each match, he mused, maybe he should take up a more sedate hobby, such as all-in wrestling.

There was something about a white ceiling, he decided, that enabled the mind to wander off. Perhaps it was the mental equivalent of a blank canvas. As soon as he began to study it the events and problems of the week came flooding back, giving him much to chew over.

Barry, in particular, was vexing him. On the one hand, Tim Beasley had seemingly provided David with clear evidence that the man was a guilty as a fox in a hen house, but on the other, David's gut instinct told him otherwise. Either Barry was a consummate liar, or something very unusual had happened. The correct thing to do, surely, was to inform Donald and Reg at the earliest opportunity and let *them* sort it out. Maybe they could arrange to borrow a polygraph machine and wire Barry to it, or perhaps even hire Dick's sister Nancy to hypnotize him and extricate the truth that way. Knowing her, she'd probably insist on at least six sessions before an answer could be provided. Something about Tim's evidence was gnawing at David, but he couldn't work out precisely what and why it was worrying him. It just was. David didn't need the keystone cops muddying the waters just yet. He needed more time to contemplate.

It was, however, impossible to allocate too much thinking time to the Barry Suggs case, largely due to the fact that David's mind had around twenty other problems vying for pole position. Sometimes, when his head felt particularly overcrowded, it helped to write a few notes in his jotting pad. Occasionally, just seeing them all listed would somehow clarify things and spark a bit of creative thinking which might, in turn, lead to a solution. To this end, he grabbed his pad and a pencil and began to write.

1. Two Aussies in loo are trying to steal our Ashes. Fact.

2. I have to thwart them for good of country. Laz will help.

3. Trilby is their boss. He can't possibly know that I know about his plan. Good!

4. I made a pig's ear of Trilby meeting, causing massive rod for my own back. Not so good.

5. Trilby now thinks I am barking mad. V. Embarrassing.

6. National Gallery has a faked Van Gogh. If they find out, I am dead meat. Now that the ratbag Trilby has made contact with them, things could get complex.

7. I have been robbed. I am down one Rolex, but at least the real Van Gogh is safely back with me. Good!

8. But how the hell do I get it back to National Gallery? Bad!

9. Tim's client, who I believe looks like Barry Suggs but is not him, now has a faked Van Gogh. Where will that end up, I wonder?

10. Barry Suggs has lost his motorbike.

11. Laz has lost his Porsche and the two Aussies have nicked his fifty quid.

12. Dick Nibbells has lost his caravan. None of this can be coincidental, surely.

13. Pauline is still acting strangely, according to Ryan, weeks after the ice-cream tub incident. Is this of importance?

14. Why are all the thefts tied in with the cricket club?

15. Can I trust Donald and Reg when I drop the bombshell? Will their loyalty to a fellow copper over-ride their sense of duty?

David studied his list. It didn't help one bit. He laid it to one side and was staring at the white ceiling again, looking for divine inspiration, when the studio doorbell rang. He slowly lifted his old, creaking bones off the settee and hobbled towards the door. He could tell by the two silhouettes in the frosted glass that it was the Securigard boys, so he opened the door to greet them, signed the chitty and took delivery of a plywood box measuring approximately a foot square. The picture within was obviously a small religious icon or triptych maybe - he just hoped that the repair did not involve the removal of a badly drawn willy and testicles. That, he felt, would be near enough the last straw.

He bade farewell to the two gentlemen and carried the box over to his cutting board, where he carefully removed the outer protection. Inside was another box made of mahogany, with dovetail joints. It had a lid, which was held on with two brass hinges, and at the front there were two ornate brass catches and a keyhole, complete with small key. Whatever he'd been sent, it was packaged beautifully. Perhaps, he thought, it could be a Nicholas Hilliard miniature, or a maybe a small and precious icon from some Russian church. Taped to the top of the old box was a letter from Mr Nicholls, addressed to David. He put it to one side and gently lifted the lid. A little shiver of excitement coursed through his body as he did so. This was always the best part of his job; seeing for the first time what he had been sent to restore.

And then he froze.

The interior of the box was padded and covered with green, slightly threadbare velvet, with a fitted section in the base of the box that was designed to hold the piece still and protect it from knocks.

Sitting snugly in its bespoke velvet bed was a small brown urn attached to a turned, lightwood plinth. A faded piece of paper had been crudely glued to the front, with a poem of sorts printed on it.

David could not have been more in awe had he been asked to restore the Holy Grail. He was looking at The Ashes.

* * *

Had a fly on the wall been observing David at precisely nine-fifteen a.m., it would have noted that the subject appeared to be transfixed by the contents of an old mahogany box and was frozen to the spot. The same fly, if asked by its superiors to file an up-to-the-minute report at nine-twenty-six a.m., would have probably signalled back with an economical 'ditto', given up the ghost and flitted off elsewhere. Had the fly been a little more patient, however, he would have been rewarded with a bit of action. The subject under observation had finally awoken from his dream, Sleeping Beauty-like, and was dialing his friend Laz. The conversation, for the benefit of the errant insect, went thus:

"Laz, what are you doing right now?"

"I was trying to do a bit of toast before some turd interrupted me."

Laz wasn't a morning person.

"Well someone as rotund as you shouldn't eat again until he's twelve stone. Get round here now. There's something you'll want to see. I'll cook you some bacon if that'll help."

"And how will I get there? Some bastard borrowed my car, remember?"

"Walk. Run even. You need the exercise. Look, stay there. I'll fetch you."

Fifteen minutes later the two friends stood staring at the urn together, in silent reverence. It was Laz who spoke first.

"But why? What's it doing here? Is it real, or just someone's idea of a joke?"

"Oh, it's real alright," replied David, slowly shaking his head from side to side, like the polar bear at Dudley Zoo always did. The difference was, the bear was bored to distraction, whereas David's head-shaking was caused by blank disbelief. "I read the letter that came with it. Graham Gunmore Nicholls runs the museum at Lord's. I was recommended by Henry at the National Gallery as a restorer of priceless works of art, and I suppose the Ashes come under that heading. He needed someone who

104

wouldn't be fazed by the importance of the thing – someone who was used to working on pictures that cost millions without the old hands shaking. But here's the curious thing. I'm shaking just looking at it, and I've retouched a Michelangelo. Mind you, I nearly shit myself working on that too, come to think of it. I suppose it's because this isn't my usual kind of thing. I restore art, not urns."

"So what's the problem with it anyway?" asked Laz. "It looks a bit, well, insignificant as trophies go, but in decent nick, considering."

"Ah!" frowned David. "The X Rays show us the answer to that." He passed Laz the evidence. "You see there? There's a nasty split where the urn is fixed to the plinth and they reckon it's getting worse. It's been repaired once before, but it was a bit of a botch job. They're frightened it might literally fall in half soon, unless I can put it right."

"And can you, old pal?"

"I think so. Listen, Laz, it goes without saying - this is top secret. Don't even tell Annie. The only reason this has been sent here is because the National Gallery told Nicholls that my place was full of state-of-the-art security. If the bloke ever found out that Van Goghs regularly disappear from under my nose, I'd be skinned alive."

"It will go no further," Laz assured him. "Bloody exciting though, eh?"

"That's an understatement, mate! I might pop over to Alton Towers after work and ride the roller coaster, just to relax myself."

David closed the box and invited Laz to join him for a spot of breakfast. Over a bacon sandwich and a pot of tea, the ramifications of this latest bombshell began to surface.

"You realize that the Lord's test is next week, don't you?" asked Laz, stealing the discarded bits of fat and rind from David's plate.

"I do!" replied David. "And Trilby is sending his henchmen to steal the Ashes on the sixteenth."

"So that's brilliant! If the Ashes are here in Stourbridge, they can't steal them can they?"

"That's what I thought, but unfortunately, one of the conditions of accepting this restoration is that I have to have it done in time for the test. There'll be thousands of museum visitors that week, and they want it on show."

"Shit!" hissed Laz. "The timing's terrible."

David had to agree. "The time is out of joint. O cursed spite, that ever I was born to set it right."

"Who said that?"

"Me, just."

"Who else?"

"Shakespeare."

"I knew it would either be him, Oscar Wilde or bloody Churchill."

David began to pace the room like a caged tiger. "It's ironic, isn't it? We have the actual Ashes right here, but I have to return them just in time for bloody Trilby's stooges to nick off with them. This has changed nothing, vis-à-vis our plans. We still have to go to London and try to catch those two in the act."

"Not necessarily," said Laz, chewing a thoughtful bacon sandwich. "You could fake the Ashes."

"WHAT?"

"You heard me. Fake it."

"Is that your answer to absolutely everything? You got me to fake the blasted Van Gogh as well. I'll end up doing thirty years without the option. I'm too pretty to go to jail. They'll rape me and abuse me. Sod off, if you'll excuse the pun."

"You won't go to jail for saving a national treasure from being stolen and returned to Australia, man. You'll be a hero, if anything. Think about it."

"I have done, bugger off!"

"Think again, cretin. If you take the *real* Ashes back to Lord's, and we don't manage to thwart those two, and they get away with it, you'll be a social pariah – a hissing and a byword. People will turn their faces away in Wollaston post office. Enville will tear up your membership in disgust. Imagine it."

"We could tell the police instead of getting involved ourselves," suggested David. "I'll tell the Birmingham rozzers and they can investigate Trilby. That's a thought. We're out of the loop then."

Laz gave David one of his exasperated looks. "Talk sense! The police will close ranks. Besides, who'd believe you? You must admit that your story is laughable. You overhear two blokes in a karzhi plotting to steal the Ashes for the Chief Superintendent of the Met. It's so crazy, you couldn't make it up!"

"I didn't need to."

"If you told that to the Chief Super in Brum, he'd laugh you out of his office."

"What, just like Trilby did, when I told him about the Black Penis Gang?"

"Exactly! But that *was* nonsense, of course."

"I'm not even sure about that now. I'm getting confused myself about what's real and what I've invented."

"Look!" said Laz, doing his best to be patient. "We're saddled with this. It's something we have to do ourselves. We'll try to catch the thieves red-handed, but it makes sense to reduce the stakes in our favour. *If* they get away with it, Trilby will disappear

107

back to Australia with a worthless replica. Then you can produce the real thing, save the day and modestly announce, "It was nothing," at the press conference held in your honour."

David wasn't convinced. "I still can't understand why a respectable copper would end his career like that in order to run off with a trophy. It doesn't make any sense to me."

"I agree," said Laz, helping himself to more tea. "We can only speculate as to his reasons. Perhaps he's mad. Maybe a childhood interest in the ownership of the trophy has grown and festered like a cancer and taken over his very being. Who can say? People in positions of power do strange things. You only have to look at King what's-his-name. He lands the top job and decides to pack it in to marry that Mrs Thingy. She'd got a face like a busted frog. I wouldn't have quit as manager of the local Asda to marry that. The facts are, those two ratbags will steal the Ashes on the sixteenth, and they're definitely stealing them for one M.J.Trilby esquire, a fellow Australian. Ours is not to reason why. Ours is to do and hopefully not die in the process. So fake that urn and get on with it."

"Can I finish my tea first?" asked David wearily.

Laz's less than sympathetic response was mercifully drowned out by the sound of David's studio doorbell. He quickly closed the mahogany box and hid it in one of his many cupboards before opening the front door. He was greeted by Donald and Reg.

"Morning Dave," smiled Donald, "We are trained to sniff out bacon sarnies from up to two miles. Can we come in?"

"Of course," replied David. "Isn't that cannibalism though, you eating bacon?"

Reg looked nonplussed – his standard reaction to virtually everything. Donald, the marginally brighter half of the partnership, reacted with a less than hearty "Har flippin' har!"

"Do come in officers," said David, somewhat belatedly, as they were already sniffing around the kitchenette area like bloodhounds. "You know Laz don't you?"

Laz waved at them from over by David's drawing board and grinned his best cheesy grin.

"Ah, the very man!" enthused Donald, delighted. "You were our next port of call. We've found your Porsche, Mr Homer."

Laz bounded over, colliding with David's coffee table and sending magazines sliding all over the floor. "Fantastic! Is it trashed? Stereo ripped out? Music tapes missing? Break it to me gently, lads."

"No, it's fine. The thief even left your tapes, but having gone through them myself, I can see why. Hardly easy listening is it?"

"Music isn't supposed to be easy to listen to, in my humble opinion."

Reg continued to look nonplussed and chewed his gum vigorously, like a football manager does when his team is getting a good kicking.

"Where *was* the car anyway?" Laz continued, puffing and blowing with the sheer relief of it all.

"It was in a lock-up garage over the Queensway. This bloke's neighbour, who's one of these Neighbourhood Watch busybodies, spotted him hiding it away in there late last night. The bloke's covered in misspelt tattoos, wears a sweaty old vest and works as a bog cleaner for the council. Nothing against bog cleaners of course, but they don't usually drive around in poncy Porsche nine-eleven pimp-mobiles - no offence Mr Homer."

"Plenty taken. And he'd nicked it from my house, this bog cleaner bloke?"

"No. It transpires that he really did buy it in a pub near Dudley for five grand. The thief asked for fifteen, which is a joke in itself, but our bog cleaner hadn't got that sort of money and offered him five. He reckoned the thief reluctantly took it, like he was desperate."

"And what did the thief look like?" asked David, doing his best to affect a nonchalant air as he snipped the rind off six more rashers of bacon. "Did the bog cleaner describe him?"

"Yes," replied Donald, "He was most helpful once we'd reminded him that he could be looking at five years and the possible confiscation of his tattoos. He said the man was tall and sporty-looking, with wiry hair and a moustache. He reckoned he was called Barry something or other."

"Shit!" said David.

"What?"

"Oh, nothing. Look lads. I had some good news for you about the painting that was stolen. I found it, and it's now safe at the gallery again. The thief had tried to get it restored by an art student that I know - Van Goghs don't tend to sell as well with knobs drawn on them – and I volunteered to do it for him. By an incredible stroke of luck, I managed to get it back. My student described the thief as tall, with wiry hair and a moustache, and said his name was Barry Suggs, who is the Enville cricket captain, but something didn't ring true. I know Barry, and if he's the Van Gogh thief, I'm a Dutchman. I didn't tell you right away, because I did a bit of investigating of my own. Barry is a crime victim too, and the way he was waxing lyrical about the thieves and what he'd like to do to them, he's either telling the truth or he's a better actor than Dustin Hoffmann."

"I don't think he's a good actor," said Reg, suddenly waking after years of sleep.

"Who, Barry?" asked David.

"No, Dustin Hoffmann."

"Well I *do*, actually," said David, "but that's neither here nor

110

there. After I heard your tale just now, I had no alternative but to tell you about him. I even thought it might be someone with a grudge against Barry who looked like him and was pretending to be him, but that seems a bit far fetched."

"Unlike the rest of this saga," added Laz, as he put the kettle on.

"Funny you should mention Barry," said Donald. "We went to see him too, about the theft of his Kawasaki, and I agree with you, David. He comes over as a nice, honest chap, but so did Crippen, probably. We can't ignore all this evidence, lads. Either Barry has a stunt double or it's him, I'm afraid."

"Well don't mention that I tipped you off," begged David, "or my chances of playing first team cricket will be nil."

"No change there then," said Laz to no one in particular, as he poured the teas.

Once breakfast was concluded, the crockery washed and Reg was sleeping nicely, Donald remembered why he'd decided to pay David a visit.

"We had a call from your friend, Chief Superintendent Trilby," he began. The blood that lived in David's face emigrated south without leaving a forwarding address.

"Oh!"

"Yes. You trouble him you know. I had to sympathize with the Chief Super on that one. You've troubled me for years. When you gamboled into his life recently, telling tales of stolen Van Goghs plastered in felt pen whatsits, he quite rightly worried about your sanity, and phoned us to check you out. I put my career on the line by sticking up for you and confirming that you were what you said you were. Being the thorough type, he rang the National Gallery pretending to be your golfing buddy and spoke to a Henry Tibbatts, who also confirmed who you were, but then dropped a Spaniard in the works by informing him that the Van Gogh in question was safely hanging on their wall. He also said he'd never heard of the Black Penis Gang. Before, old Trilby thought you were a loony who *thought* he was a famous art restorer and had invented some crazy story about a gang of art thieves for no apparent reason. *Now*, after his conversation with Henry, he thinks you are a loony who really *is* an art restorer and has invented some crazy story about a gang of art thieves for no apparent reason. As you can see, your standing in the eyes of the Chief Super has improved out of all proportion. Now he's phoned me again and wants answers. So have you got any?"

David paced the floor in order to give himself time to concoct one of his patented fabrications. Luckily, this one came quite quickly.

"Erm, yes. I didn't want to alarm the National Gallery or be late for their deadline, so I sent them a replica which I painted myself, just to give me time to think. This was the picture that Henry told Trilby about. In the interim period, I rescued the original, as I explained earlier, and returned it to the gallery. I, erm, didn't want Henry to think that my studio leaked Van Goghs left, right and centre, so I told a little white lie. I said that I'd cocked up the removal of the penis, so to speak, and it had needed to be redone, so I faked the picture in order that he'd have something to hang on the wall in time for the Van Gogh exhibition. As soon as I got the original back, I took it to London and swapped them over. Henry was a bit miffed, but saw that I'd done it so as not to let him down, you see. As to the Black Penis Gang, well, erm, that was only a theory that we restorers believed, and we didn't want to frighten the gallery unnecessarily until we could, erm, prove it, so Henry wouldn't have known what Trilby was on about."

David walked over to his cupboards as he spoke and opened the one containing the original Van Gogh.

"Look," he smiled, pulling out the picture to show to the officer, "here's my faked one. As you can see, it's hardly the same standard as the original, when you look at it closely."

Donald scrutinized the painting with his expert artist's eye.

"Christ, Dave, you're right. It's dog rough, mate. Look at all those ugly thick lumps of paint, just daubed on. I'm surprised you got away with it."

David replaced the painting, and tried to dampen the smirk that was spreading like wildfire across his face.

"So as you can see, there's always a logical explanation!"

Donald seemed satisfied with this, and vowed to put the Chief Super right. He gave Reg a gentle kick to the shins which woke him with a start. After a brief discussion about police brutality, they headed for the door, taking a delighted Laz with them in order that he could be re-united with his car.

"And once we've sorted Mr Homer out," said Donald, "Reg and I will be paying another visit to Barry Suggs." And with that, they were gone.

No sooner had David taken the mahogany box out of the cupboard and placed it on his desk, than the doorbell rang again. He opened the door to the postman, who had a package to be signed for. As David handed the document to him, he realized that this was not the regular man with whom he often shared the odd bawdy joke, middle-aged gripe or pithy observation. This new fellow was, as near as damn it, Dick Nibbells in a postie's hat. The similarity was too strong to ignore, so David didn't.

"You're not related to a bloke named Dick Nibbells are you?" he asked.

"Cousin," replied the verbally frugal postie.

"You look just like him," observed David.

"I know," replied the postie.

"Sorry to hear about his bad luck."

"What, looking like me?"

This was good, thought David. He was opening up. That was four words, and a touch of humour. He'd be up to the regular postie's standard in a decade or two.

"No, about his caravan, I mean."

"His caravan?"

"Yeah. It's been stolen."

"It hasn't."

"It has, apparently."

"It hasn't. He hasn't got one."

Chapter 12

Harry the Potter

This startling revelation had left David staring into space again. He seemed to spend an inordinate amount of time doing that lately, and it was wasting huge slabs of his life. He eventually wrenched himself out of his coma and phoned his old friend Harry, the potter.

"Excuse me if I sound distracted," he explained, "but life is even more complex than usual at the moment. Look, H, I need you to do something for me in a hell of a hurry, if you can."

"Fair enough," replied H, "but I have to warn you, I've put my rates up this month."

"Put them up?" asked David, reeling. "As far as I can recall, they've always been up!"

He described to Harry what was needed, omitting to mention where his handiwork would eventually end up. Instead, he offered the rather weak explanation that his budgerigar, Botham, had finally dropped off its perch and the Ashes replica was to be its final resting place. Harry bought it hook, line and sinker, which was hardly surprising. On reflection, it sounded far more credible than the true version. David spent the rest of the morning preparing an exact scale drawing and a precise colour sample. He could hardly show Harry the real thing, after all.

Once this was completed, he rang Laz to see if he'd taken possession of his car. Laz was elated, and still couldn't quite believe that he'd gotten away so lightly. David prided himself on being perceptive, and had made a Sherlock Holmes-like assumption, based on the merest of clues, that Laz was puffing away on a cigarette as they spoke.

"Did you just exhale some smoke then?" he demanded.

"No!" replied Laz indignantly, "I just ran to the phone, and I was just a little bit, erm, out of breath."

"Out of breath because of smoking, probably. That wasn't an out of breath-type breath, it was a 'blow some smoke out of the corner of your mouth' type of breath. Own up, buster!"

"Well, okay, if you have to know, I was having a quiet celebratory fag, not that it's any of your business, with your bloody on-line Big Brother-style interrogation."

"Ah, but it is my business, chimney breath," retorted David. "We have a wager, unless you've forgotten."

"I haven't forgotten, and this was just a momentary blip on the radar, or whatever the bloody expression is. When my course is finished, I have every confidence that my addiction will be cured. At the moment, I'm only halfway into the treatment, so the occasional fag is allowed. How's your batting coming on? Reached double figures yet?"

This was meant to sting, and it did.

"Actually, no, but Barry reckons I'm improving daily. I wouldn't be counting your winnings yet, if I were you, fag-ash Lil."

And with that, he replaced the receiver. For no apparent reason, a thought flitted across his mind. It dashed so quickly that David could not make out what it was. It seemed to dart hither and thither, like a soldier running for cover and trying not to get hit by

116

a sniper. David stared out of the window again, hoping against hope that the little thought would scamper back again, this time more slowly, so that he could catch a glimpse of him. For fully five minutes, the thought remained hidden amongst the grey matter, and then, like a frightened rabbit, it bolted again, pausing just long enough in the middle of David's head to be identified. Whereupon, quite suddenly, the tiny, insignificant little thought blossomed and exploded into a multi-coloured fireworks display.

David had just had one of his eureka moments.

He reached for a pencil and began to doodle on the corner of his layout pad. This always helped him to crystallize his thoughts, and on this occasion, the technique did not let him down. Slowly, the pieces of the jigsaw began to interlock, though what they were spelling out, if true, were bizarre in the extreme. He began to compile one of his infamous lists.

1. Connections. Van Gogh and Rolex stolen. No one knew about painting except Laz and Suzanne.

2. Laz's Porsche stolen. There's a Laz connection again.

3. Kawasaki stolen. Cricket club connection.

4. Caravan stolen. Cricket club again. There is no caravan, according to monosyllabic postie. Why would Nibbells pretend to have a caravan stolen?

5. To deflect blame maybe? He paints himself as another victim. Clever!

6. The Barry Suggs conundrum. If it wasn't Suggsy, it could be Nibbells, which means that Nibbells is trying to lay blame on Suggsy, but how and why?

7. Another connection. Baz and Laz are both being treated by Nibbell's sister.

David's list had been productive, but now, suddenly, he had hit a brick wall. If it wasn't Suggs who had handed over the painting to Dim Tim, it blooming well looked like him, at least according to Tim. Presuming the lad wasn't viewing his client through one of those fairground mirrors that turns a little fat man into a tall, wiry one and adds a moustache in the process, it was safe to assume that Tim's client looked at least a little like Suggs. That ruled out Nibbells, unless he had an accomplice, of course. Then there was the question of why Nibbells would want to lay the blame on Suggs. Did he have a long-standing grudge, perhaps? Maybe Suggs had copped him in the box with a ninety-mile-per-hour corker which had prevented him from fathering children. That wouldn't cause a rift, surely? These cricketers tended to forgive and forget minor stuff like that after a swift half in the pavilion, and Barry himself said he'd no enemies that he knew of. He didn't seem the enemy-making type.

Then there was the question of how Nibbells could have known about the Van Gogh, if indeed it was him. The only person who knew about that was Laz, and he wouldn't tell a soul. David would stake his life on it.

Unless.

Unless Laz had *unwittingly* told someone that his spare Porsche ignition key was under Dennis Taylor the garden gnome, and that there was a Van Gogh in David's studio. Maybe Barry too, had *unwittingly* revealed the whereabouts of his Kawasaki keys.

Dick Nibbells had a sister who could do that – coax things out of the victim without them being aware of it. The idea was so far-fetched as to be preposterous, but it was feasible. There would have to be three of them involved. Dick himself, who lied about his caravan to paint himself as a fellow victim, his sister, the hypnotist, who could surely extract information whilst they were under the influence, and a person, as yet unidentified, who bore a striking resemblance to Barry Suggs. In fact, it didn't even need to be a striking resemblance, now that David had given it a little more thought. Any wiry-haired, moustachioed, athletic-looking man would do. The only piece of the jigsaw that was missing now was the motive for blaming poor old Barry, but that would surely become evident once Donald and Reg had beaten it out of them.

David reached for the phone. He wanted to try his theory out on Donald, but he realized that doing so would be roughly comparable to a science teacher endeavouring to explain Einstein's Theory of Relativity to a goldfish.

* * *

Harry the Potter wasn't everyone's idea of a dream date, it had to be said. His beard made Darwin's look like a five o'clock shadow, and several of its more remote outposts seemed to have declared independence with a view to colonizing his nostrils and ears. As if this wasn't bad enough, Harry's penchant for Severn Valley Railway steam trains, finger in the ear folk music and filthy fingernails ensured that women gave him a wide berth, which was probably how he preferred it. Until he found a soul mate who actually enjoyed polishing brass lamps while she listened to The Spinners' Greatest Hits, Harry would continue to find far more pleasure in stoking some old boiler than - well, stoking some old boiler.

Sartorial he was not, and David couldn't imagine a worse scenario than spending a harsh Canadian winter with him, holed up in a bleak log cabin in the woods, but boy, could he fire a pot, and his latest offering did not disappoint. David held it carefully, examining it from all angles, and it was obvious that Harry the Potter had worked his magic once more. He'd even turned a perfect replica of the plinth in exactly the same shade and species of wood as the original. The urn needed ageing, of course, and the inscription and contents were still missing, but as a starting point,

119

it was incredible. David doubted that even Graham Gunmore-Nicholls would have spotted the difference, once the ace restorer and forger had added his own magical finishing touches.

David thanked Harry profusely, greased his filthy palm with silver and flung him out sharpish, in order that he could get down to business. Touchingly, Harry remarked, as he trotted down the studio steps, that in his opinion, it was a special kind of person who would lavish that kind of attention, not to mention cash, on a humble budgie. David affected a look that perfectly combined piety, deep sadness and modesty, before explaining that Botham had been with them for over thirty years and was part of the family. Nor was this mere fabrication on his part. There had, once upon a time, been a budgerigar, but its life had been cruelly cut short after a mere four years and it had ended up in the pedal bin.

David was not usually so quick to dispatch his suppliers, but time was at a premium. The urn had to be back by the morning of the sixteenth, so that Graham could have it installed in the museum once more, ready to greet the test match punters. David had suggested that he could return the urn in person, as he was travelling to the St John's Wood area that very day on business. This, quite understandably, was met with an unequivocal 'No thank you', and the Securigard van was ordered. Though David was obviously unable to share his thoughts with Mr Gunmore-Nicholls, he couldn't help finding the whole situation quite bizarre. A Police Chief Superintendent was arranging for his two henchmen to steal the Ashes on the sixteenth, and David was beavering away trying to fake them and get them reinstated at Lord's in time for the robbers to steal them. He now had the real Ashes in his old cupboard where he kept the coffee tin, and an original Van Gogh. How he got himself into these situations he would never know. Maybe his doting mother had accidentally dropped him on his head as a child. Whatever the reason, at least life was rarely dull, and he was thankful for that, if nothing else.

As the sixteenth approached, David became more and more

stressed. He called a meeting of the war council with Laz on the fifteenth, so that they could decide on a plan of attack. If they were to stand a chance of thwarting the Australians, the day had to be organized with military precision.

However, first on the agenda was the Dick Nibbells situation. David mooted his rather outlandish theory about the three conspirators while Laz listened intently, but could add nothing. He'd known about the Van Gogh and told no one, but he obviously couldn't vouch for what he may or may not have said whilst under the ether. It was best, they both agreed, to leave all that in the incapable hands of Donald and Reg, and see what turned up after a bit of police brutality. Next up for discussion was catching Mervin and Brett red-handed. The scribbled note that Laz had found told them precisely when the two men planned to rob the museum, which was a help, and both Laz and David could easily identify them, but the Lord's ground was large and would be swimming with visitors. How they could cover several exits at the same time was proving to be more problematic. They needed to prowl the perimeter and somehow communicate as they did so. At this point, David had one of his many brainwaves. He invited Laz to follow him into the living room, where Suzanne was playing at shops with Lauren and her dolls.

"Lauren," said David, smiling sweetly, "can Daddy borrow your walkie-talkies tomorrow? The ones Santa bought you for Christmas?"

"No, Daddy," said Lauren.

David was understandably taken aback, but continued regardless.

"Oh! Why not? Daddy will look after them. It's very important."

"I need them, Daddy. Toby is coming to play with me."

David looked askance at Suzanne. "Toby? Now she's bringing

men back to the house. Do we know his parents? What does the dad earn? Has this been going on long?"

Suzanne looked at the ceiling. "He goes to school with her. He's a lovely lad. I can't believe you just said that!"

"It was a joke, dear. Next time I'll send it to you in an envelope with JOKE written on it, just so as you don't misunderstand. Just for one day, please Lauren? You can play with the dolls instead, or the Wendy house."

"Will you get me one of those things that I can wind up then?"

"She's already got one. It's called a dad," suggested Laz.

David was horrified. His little girl was already picking up underhand bartering and shopping skills from her mother. It would only be a matter of time until she was examining the clothes in his wardrobe and telling him they were frayed.

"She's on about a wind-up dog that can walk and it really poos. You have to get it up with a little plastic pooper-scoop."

"Tasteful," commented Laz. "Is it real poo or just little plastic things?"

"Plastic, I hope," replied David. "Lord knows what happens when all the poops have come out. I suppose you have to load the dog up, like a BB gun, so it can fire them out again."

"I was never blessed with children," said Laz, for no obvious reason.

"Okay then, Lauren," sighed David, "Lend me the walkie-talkies and I'll get you the wind-up doggy, but I don't want to find poo all over Daddy's carpets when I get in at night. We have enough trouble with Hoover over there."

Hoover the spaniel raised her head briefly to acknowledge her name and then fell asleep again. David walked over to Lauren's toy box, extricated the surveillance equipment and beat a hasty retreat back to the sanctity of the Fortress of Solitude. He handed Laz his walkie-talkie and began to explain how it was operated.

"Whoa!" said Laz, swiftly handing it back.

"What?"

"I point-blank refuse to wander around the perimeter of Lord's holding a pink walkie-talkie with Barbie written on it."

David put his foot down. "Laz, you have to."

"It's a bloody toy. It won't work, man. Can't we go and buy a couple of mobile phones? My mate Jim's got one, and a few of the lads at the factory have started to use them."

"There's no time for that now," insisted David, "and anyway, the walkie-talkies *do* work. Me and Suzanne tried them out before we, erm, let Santa have them, and they're brilliant. They work up to a hundred yards, really well."

"I am not talking into a Barbie walkie-talkie - full stop. We'll have to think of Plan B."

"Okay, okay!" David conceded. He opened up his London A to Z and began to circle key areas with his biro. Ideally, he would have preferred to have been in an underground bunker, studying a much larger, table-mounted map with model tanks and magnetic flags on it, but sadly this wasn't feasible.

"So I drive to the multi-storey, here, and park up. The ground is just here, and on Mervin and Brett's map, they mention 'rear exit', so you stand in this street here, and I'll wander around by the front entrance, just in case they pass that way and you miss them. If you spot them either coming or going, contact me by walkie-talkie and we'll tail them. .."

"I am not talking into a pink Barbie walkie-talkie."

"Okay. I heard that already. We'll play it by ear. The important thing is to trail them, see where they end up."

"Brilliant! Then what?"

"Well, I don't know about you, but I don't fancy getting into a fist fight with two burly Australians, so I've had an idea, and don't laugh. I phoned Donald the other day about my Dick Nibbells theory, as you know, and while we were talking, I asked for his considered opinion on a possible scenario, stressing that it was just hypothetical, of course. I asked him how the Midlands police would react if they found out that, say, a senior officer in another force was corrupt, and his answer encouraged me no end. Once I'd explained what 'hypothetical' and 'scenario' meant, he was most forthcoming. He said, and I quote, 'We'd nail the bugger, especially if it was someone from the Met, because they're bloody la-di-da superior bastards who think they're 'it', just because they patrol the bloody capital'. Well, as you can imagine, this gave me heart. I propose that we find where the Aussies are staying and then let Donald and Reg in on our little plan. They can sneak up to London incognito, arrest them, charge them with stealing the Ashes and nicking fifty quid off you, and brutally interrogate them until they spill the beans on old Trilby, which they will if it means avoiding a long stretch. The West Mids cops will then arrest Trilby, thereby scoring a major victory over their bitter rivals. Donald and Reg get promoted, thanks to the huge scalp I promised them and then delivered, and everything's rosy. What do you think?"

Laz weighed this. "Fair enough, I suppose," he replied, "but what if we just don't spot the two Aussies and they nick off with the Ashes? Have you considered that?"

"Of course," said David. "If they do manage to steal the thing from under our noses, it's only a replica anyway. If the worst comes to the worst, I produce the real urn and tell them that I was aware of the plan all along, and that's why I replicated the thing. Either way, we come out of this smelling good! It's a win-win situation, my dear old friend. How on earth can we fail?"

Chapter 13

Unlucky For Some

It was six-thirty a.m. on the sixteenth of June and David was tossing and turning with the stress of it all. Eventually, Suzanne insisted that he get up and make a pot of tea, as he'd managed to pull all the bed clothes off her at least nine times. He duly did so, partly so that he could take a look at his and Harry's urn again, and make sure that it was absolutely perfect before the Securigard lads arrived at half-eight. Nor did the final inspection disappoint. David was far too modest a restorer to use the word 'perfection', but in his heart of hearts, he knew it was as near as made no difference. Besides which, the last thing that either Henry Tibbatts or Graham Gunmore-Nicholls would be looking for, on receipt of one of David's restorations, was a forgery. He placed the replica inside its velvet-lined box and carefully hid the real urn in his cupboard, next to the Van Gogh. What with all the excitement, he hadn't had time to actually restore the original urn, but from what he could see, it wasn't a complex job, by his standards at least, and he could turn his attention to it once the drama of the day was over.

David took Suzanne a cup of tea in bed and then showered and dressed. Whilst still halfway through his second round of toast, he decided to ring Laz, just to check if everything was still okay and all systems go. This was probably not a wise move, as Laz was notoriously anti-morning, and possibly the nearest thing that the pub and restaurant refurbishing industry had got to Keith Richards. He'd *heard* of seven-thirty a.m., of course, but had never before actually experienced it. Having already slung his alarm clock at the wall in a rage, because it had dared to do what he himself had programmed it to do on the previous evening, he was in no mood for unnecessary intrusions.

"We arranged all this yesterday, you bloody cretin," he snarled, "so why you have to check up on me in the middle of the night is beyond me."

David refused to take this onslaught personally. He'd seen documentaries about what drug addicts were like when they didn't get their fix. Laz would be fine once he'd had his first cup of coffee and a fag. He just felt sorry for the poor woman who was lying next to him.

The Securigard men were thankfully bang on time, and it was with his premier vital organ lodged just behind his teeth and beating dysrhythmically, that David signed the paperwork and watched his creation disappear. Externally, the urn looked perfect. He just hoped that no one at Lord's could deduce from an X-ray that the contents consisted mainly of ash and minute particles of sausage from the next-door neighbour's barbecue.

David kissed a totally unconcerned Lauren and a slightly worried Suzanne goodbye, gathered up his coat and car keys and quietly left the house. Laz, true to form, was nowhere near ready, and, according to Annie, had spent at least half an hour washing one arm at the bathroom sink, in a kind of dull stupor. After much cajoling and harrying, he eventually joined his jittery companion in the Mercedes and they set off for the big city.

Though Laz had patiently explained to David at least three times that London would only take them an hour and three-quarters – two on a bad day – David, being David, had insisted that they set off really, really early, just in case. They arrived at the multi-storey car park just after half past eleven, meaning that they had several hours to kill, and though Laz maintained a dignified silence throughout, his face said 'I told you so.' David sensed that his friend had got the hump about having to be dragged kicking and screaming from his pit, and argued that, had he allowed him to wash both of his arms *and* his face, they'd still have been in Stourbridge at teatime. Begrudgingly conceding that this was a fair point, Laz dragged himself out of his grumpy mood and suggested a second breakfast at the first café they could find, followed by a quick sight-seeing tour. The car park was only a ten minute walk from Lord's, so they headed for the ground where they found a small café not far from the front entrance. David chose the bacon sandwich on brown toast with a cup of tea, and Laz ordered the full English with extra fried bread and a mug of coffee, which he consumed while poring over a borrowed copy of the Sun. After plastering most of the naked women within with dollops of grease and tomato juice, he returned the paper to the rack, ready for the next customer to enjoy.

Breakfast concluded, they sportingly tossed a coin to see who would pay, and David lost. Once his appeal for best of three had been firmly rejected, he strolled to the counter, only to realize that, in his excitement, he had completely forgotten to bring any cash with him. He did, however, have his cheque book, so he paid up, slipped to the lavatory and met his friend just outside the café.

Laz was keen to visit nearby Abbey Road, where the Beatles recorded their albums, and particularly wanted to walk across the famous zebra crossings that featured on the eponymous album, Abbey Road. He even suggested removing his shoes and socks, as Paul had done, but David feared this would not only stop the traffic, but also render any passing pedestrians incapable, so the idea was shelved. Luckily, David always carried his Nikon camera with him, just in case he spotted a useful piece of reference material for a painting, so when they arrived at the famous crossings, he asked a passing Japanese tourist to snap them as they

127

strolled across the road. Ever the perfectionist, he left Laz standing in the middle of the crossing and irritating the hell out of the queue of impatient motorists, while he art-directed the shot, and then leapt back into the scene to join his friend. Not content with one photograph, he then ran back to the Japanese gentleman and asked him to bracket the exposures, just in case, so he could choose the best of the three frames when he developed them. By now, the car horns were belting out their warnings, but one only ever did this once, and it had to be right. Imagine if they'd travelled all that way and come home with sub-standard snaps!

It was Laz's turn to be a prima donna now, because he was trying to perfectly replicate John Lennon's stance, and he'd belatedly realized that his left arm wasn't quite in the right place. This meant that the little Nippon would have to use the little Nikon all over again, and of course, there was still the issue of bracketing the exposures to consider. David was still hollering his instructions to the gentleman, when a burly lorry driver, who had been held up as a result of this major photo shoot, vacated his cab in order to make feelings known. He was swiftly followed by a black cab driver who wished to endorse his fellow traveller's point of view, and now the little Japanese fellow was excitedly clicking away like David Bailey and shouting, "Perfek! Perfek! John, Paw, George and Lingo!"

Towards the end of their career, and especially during the making of Abbey Road, the Beatles were beginning to become a little disenchanted with each other, and heated arguments were commonplace. It seemed fitting then, in a strange way, that David's photo album would eventually display a black and white ten-by-eight shot of the four 'Beatles' almost coming to blows as they crossed the road to the studios. However, Laz was a firm believer in discretion being the better part of valour, so when the lorry driver suggested that David's Nikon was about to play a major role in an impromptu endoscopy examination, Lennon and McCartney decided to relieve the photographer of his duties and leg it in the general direction of Lord's.

After a brief detour in search of McCartney's home in St.John's Wood, followed by lunch in a pub seemingly infested by gangsters, barrow boys and ladies of the night, they fetched up at the ground once more. David and Laz synchronized watches and split up, as planned, with Laz patrolling the far end of the stadium. It was now just after four-twenty p.m., and various official-looking characters were entering or leaving the ground. But none resembled the two Australians. Ideally, David needed at least five more undercover agents to help out, due to the number of different gates, but he'd thought it unwise to confide in anyone other than Laz.

After a fruitless first hour, Laz decided to communicate with his partner on the other side of the ground and compare notes. He took Ken's purple walkie-talkie from his coat pocket and pressed the silver button.

"Ken to Barbie. Are you reading me?"

There was a crackle, followed by a fuzzy voice.

"Barbie here. Any sightings, Ken? Over."

"Not a sausage, Barbie. Could they be disguised as repairmen, like always happens in the A Team? Over."

"Could be, Ken. Give it ten minutes and call again. Over."

David was beginning to feel very silly indeed, and wondering to himself if he'd dreamed the whole thing, when he suddenly spotted someone he recognized leaving by the front gates. He buzzed Laz on his Barbie-phone with some urgency.

"Ken, come in, Ken. Red alert. Suspect spotted leaving main entrance. It's not Merv or Brett though. I'm sure it's Trilby, but in civvies, and he's carrying a plastic bag. Get over here now! Over."

129

This was unexpected. David could only speculate that something had gone wrong with Trilby's original plan. Maybe the Aussies had let him down – drunk on the job perhaps – who could say? For whatever reason, the policeman had gone it alone. Either that or all three were in the ground at the same time. Think! What to do? Trilby was carrying a bag. Maybe the two Aussies had stolen the urn and slipped it to Trilby, who was now swaggering out of the front gates with it, as bold as brass. David made a snap decision. He and Laz would ignore the two Aussies and concentrate on Trilby.

The Chief Super crossed the road and began to walk away from the ground, just as Laz rejoined David, panting and breathless.

"He's over there, heading in the direction of our café," hissed David. "Let's follow him from a discreet distance."

Chief Superintendent Trilby was indeed heading for their café. He'd been welcomed by Graham Gunmore-Nicholls, shown round the museum, and then spent a very emotional few minutes on the pitch, scattering his beloved father's ashes. Now, with tears still welling up in his eyes, he needed to get a quick cup of coffee and calm himself before returning home. He entered the café, sat down in the far corner away from the other punters and placed his plastic bag on the table. When the young waitress sidled over with her notepad he ordered a coffee – strong and nearly black. He did not notice the two gentlemen over the far side of the café, reading newspapers. He was too busy thinking about his childhood in Australia, donkey rides on his dad's back, and a million other bitter-sweet memories. After fully ten minutes of this dewy-eyed contemplation, he drained the bitter cup and headed for the lavatories, passing David and Laz as he did so. Laz immediately immersed himself in his grease-stained Sun, whilst David stared intently into his tea mug, emerging seconds later looking like Mr Magoo, with his lenses completely steamed up and unable to see.

"He's heading for the loo," hissed Laz, "What do we do now?"

"We have to snatch that bag," whispered David, "and this is the best time to do it. I'll follow him. You go to the counter, quick, and buy a massive family tub of ice-cream. The biggest one they've got. I've had an idea. Now hurry up. We don't have long!"

Laz scampered off as David tip-toed into the lavatory. He'd already been once before, so luckily, he knew the layout of the place, and he could tell right away that Trilby was in one of the two cubicles. The bottom half of the plastic bag was clearly visible beneath the locked door, and judging by the sounds emanating from behind the door, the policeman was there for a prolonged stay. Seconds later, Laz entered the lavatory with a plastic bag of his own. David immediately gestured for him to remain silent. The irony was not lost on him that the plot to steal the Ashes had been hatched in a lavatory cubicle. It seemed fitting, therefore, that his heroic scheme to rescue them should also be played out in similar surroundings. He gestured for Laz to occupy the adjoining cubicle, stand on the seat, and when given the signal, drop the tub of ice-cream onto the head of the Chief Constable as he defecated. Laz fixed David with an imploring, soul-searching kind of look – the one that a wildebeest would probably give to a fellow wildebeest after it had suggested he take on the hungry lion, one against one. David, however, remained unmoved, and responded with a vigorous pseudo-Italian hand gesture that was intended to express a sense of extreme urgency.

Taking a deep breath, Laz mounted the lavatory seat, winced, and emptied the contents of his plastic bag onto the cranium of the unsuspecting officer below.

The results were dramatic. Deep from within the cubicle, Chief Superintendent Trilby yelled, "What the bloody hell?" hastily pulled up his trousers and catapulted out of the door, just in time to see Laz's pigtail exit the room. Trilby charged after him at a rate of knots, but was badly delayed by the arrival of a large group of tourists, cluttering up the aisle. Thrusting them aside like nine-pins, the Chief Super shot out of the café, only to see an overweight man charging down the high street with his pigtail standing out horizontally behind him.

Like most Australians, Michael Trilby was naturally athletic, and though he would never see forty again, he was in very good shape, having run regularly in the police cross-country team and religiously swum a mile every day before breakfast. Laz, on the other hand, insisted on catching a cab, even when dining at his next-door neighbours, and consequently he was flagging already. Glancing back and seeing a rampaging Chief Super getting ever closer, however, seemed to give him a boost of sorts, simultaneously providing a cure for his long-standing constipation problem. Sensing that this burst of energy couldn't be sustained, he decided to play dirty, and as he shot past the Indian grocery store, he resorted to emergency tactics. He'd seen a similar scenario in just about every action film he'd ever watched, from Indiana Jones to the Italian Job, and now here was his chance to try it out. He had no desire to disrupt the honest shopkeeper's living, but these were extreme circumstances. If the policeman caught hold of him he'd be looking at five years without the option, and he had a successful business to run - he simply couldn't spare the time away from it. Gasping for air now, he tipped over the huge display of fruit and vegetables onto the pavement, and was delighted to see his pursuer come a real purler at the first hurdle. A quick backward glance revealed the hapless rozzer up to his neck in a mound of multi-coloured peppers, and looking for all the world like a child throwing a tantrum in a ball pit. This distraction gained Laz valuable seconds, which he didn't waste. The downside, however, was that now he had half of the Indian subcontinent *and* a seething police officer baying for his blood.

* * *

At the multi-storey car park, David was pacing the floor by his vehicle and fretting. It had been ages now, and there was no sign of Laz whatsoever. He was beginning to fear the worst – that his accomplice had been caught and arrested, which would have made the perfect ending for a disastrous day. When Trilby shot out of the cubicle like a greyhound from the traps, he had conveniently left his plastic bag behind, but a closer examination revealed nothing more than an empty plastic tub. This had led David to suspect that Trilby was nothing more than a decoy, or red herring, and all the time, his henchmen were getting away with the real urn. His mood lightened a little as he remembered that even the real urn wasn't the *real* urn, but this didn't make up for the fact that the two had got away scot-free, and would probably be on a plane within days. Without Mervin and Brett, David couldn't finger Trilby, and his best laid plans, as Rabbie Burns so eloquently put it, would all gang agley.

He was just about to consider the idea of ending it all in a lonely London car park by slashing both wrists with his car keys, when he saw a distant figure that he recognized rounding the entrance to level four. The sorrowful creature looked lame and was staggering towards the Mercedes like a dying donkey.

"Laz!" called out David, but Laz was just too exhausted to reply. He eventually crawled up the car and slumped onto the bonnet, his whole body heaving up and down like a beached whale. There was steam coming off his back, just like a racehorse after the Derby, and he was gasping for air like a fish deprived of water.

David decided to leave him for five minutes before he tried to communicate again. Then he let his friend have it with both barrels.

"So anyway, what on earth were you thinking of, you bloody nutter?"

"Gnah!" groaned Laz, still face down on the car's bonnet.

"What effect did you honestly think three individual mini-tubs of raspberry ripple would have on a big, strapping policeman? Mild irritation perhaps?"

"They'd only got the little tubs so I got three."

"And what bloody use did you think three would be? I wanted you to knock him unconscious, or at least stun him, not politely tap him on the back of the head. You'd have needed twenty of those to make an impression, you loony. Why didn't you fill the plastic bag full of them?"

"I didn't want to break into my twenty pound note."

"You what?"

"Well, I had the right change for three. A plastic bag full would have been a bit expensive."

"I see. So you dropped three mini-tubs of raspberry ripple on the Chief Superintendent's head, and I bet you were surprised when he wasn't unconscious straight away weren't you, you buffoon? I bet he sat there thinking, why has someone dropped these into my cubicle while I'm trying to have a shit? It doesn't get much more bloody bizarre and surreal does it?"

Laz groaned again. Ordinarily, he would have put up a spirited defence, but it was hard to rise to the occasion when his lungs felt like deflated crisp packets.

"And another thing. Where's Lauren's walkie-talkie?" asked David.

"Oh shit! I lost it when I sent the fruit and veg flying."

David sighed and ran his hands through his thinning hair in a distracted kind of way. "Now we're in *real* trouble."

* * *

Meanwhile, at forty-nine, Lettersby Avenue, Mervin and Brett were busy leaving by the back door with a small ceramic urn. The house alarm system had been turned off, as promised, and everything had gone swimmingly, thanks to Michael Trilby's home help, Caroline. She and her husband, James, had first met Mervin and Brett at one of their many cricket matches, and had chatted to them in the pavilion bar after another heavy defeat. Imagine their delight when she told them what she did to keep the wolf from the door, and then imagine their euphoria when they bumped into her again, in a romantic little Italian restaurant in Knightsbridge, with a completely different young man in tow. So stricken were they with this pretty young English rose, that they followed her home afterwards and put a little proposition to her. Either she obliged them by informing them when her employer was going to be out, turning off the alarms and going walkabout for an hour, or hubby would learn all about Giles, the smooth young estate agent with the BMW. Distraught and feeling more than a little foolish, she agreed, knowing full well that she had placed herself between Ayers Rock and a hard place.

Now that they had Trilby Senior's ashes, they intended to spend their last few days in England, watching the second test at Lord's – preferably in false beards - before flying home to collect their reward. Whether Maurice Trilby would have been quite so thrilled with them, once he discovered that he'd actually scattered the ashes of his brother's beloved police dog, Buster, into Sydney harbour, was another matter.

Chapter 14

Arachnophobia

Graham Gunmore-Nicholls shook hands and said goodbye to Chief Inspector Trilby. It was quite clear that the man was feeling a little emotional, and wanted to get on with scattering his father's ashes. Besides, Graham had a very busy schedule himself. The second test match was due to begin the following day, and Lord's was a hive of activity. He was just thinking to himself that the Securigard men were rather late, when the intercom buzzed on his desk and his secretary announced their arrival. He ushered the two gentlemen in, signed for the box, and bade them a fond farewell. Graham was old school, stiff-upper lipped and an ex-army major, but he couldn't help allowing himself a moment of schoolboy enthusiasm as he unpacked the mahogany box. He took a deep breath, unlocked the lid and slowly opened it, to reveal his beloved Ashes urn. He pulled on his white cotton gloves and gingerly lifted the urn from its green velvet bed, in order that he could inspect David's workmanship before returning the treasure to its cabinet. What he saw then froze his blood, and made each, individual hair on his neck stand to attention, like quills on the fretful porpentine. A large, black, hairy spider had made itself at home in the lush velvet bed beneath the urn, and as the relic was lifted, it made a dart for freedom, up Mr Gunmore-Nicholls's white glove. Screaming like a two-year-old, he flung the urn

136

skywards and flicked feverishly at his glove with his other hand. The urn flew through the air, as if in slow motion, while the spider did likewise in the other direction.

Spiders, after millions of years of evolution, have learnt to adapt to being flicked off gloves, and can fall what, to them, would seem like huge distances and land unscathed. They merely wince a little, dust themselves off, and scamper away at speed to the nearest skirting board. Victorian urns, however, have only been around for a relatively short time in evolutionary terms, and tend to shatter, as this one did now.

Those who have ever dropped a wine glass onto a tiled kitchen floor will appreciate the carnage beheld by the Lord's museum curator at that point. The bits seem to travel unfeasible distances, and householders can expect to find them well into the next decade. Just when they are confident that the last bit of Royal Brierley Crystal has been rounded up, a year later, another piece pops up behind the fridge. In this regard, the sacred urn did not disappoint. Every square inch of Mr Gunmore-Nicholls's office floor seemed to have a little piece of cricket history on it.

The poor curator stood and stared at the debris for some fifteen minutes in silent disbelief, a broken man. If there was a scale of brokenness in broken men, then Mr Gunmore-Nicholls was a ten. He was a broken as the urn, in fact. Only ten minutes previously, he had observed a tear from in the eye of a Chief Superintendent, and at the time he had thought the fellow weak. These police force types thought they were hard, but compared to the military, he found them wanting. Now, here he was, shedding tears of his own, and all because a twopenny-halfpenny old pot had been shattered. He was also experiencing another emotion that was a stranger to him – that of self-loathing. He had always been a confident person, but now he hated himself for being so childish about a silly little spider. In his army days he had seen action, and experienced the pinging of enemy bullets around his head. Twice wounded by snipers, he had merely requested a band-aid and asked to be allowed to continue, complaining in the strongest terms when the field hospital insisted he take ten minutes off and swallow two aspirins. Graham's arachnophobia began as a child, after his older brother, Monty, dropped a big fat spider into his mouth as he slept, and no matter how many times he confronted his fear, it would not go away. Barry Suggs, as has been well documented, had an issue with wasps, which, if anything, was far more severe than Graham's problem. The only difference was, Barry didn't carry priceless urns around on a daily basis.

When something approaching reason had returned to its throne, Graham sat at his desk and dialed the only phone number he knew that might, just might, be able to offer advice. It was a million to one shot, but there was no real alternative.

Chapter 15

An Inspector Calls Again

It was barely half-past eight when the doorbell rang, and David had barely slept, thanks to a vivid nightmare. A tribe of Aborigines had tied him to a tree and were tearing off his limbs, dipping them in some form of fat and sucking on them as they sat around a camp fire. One particularly ugly one with a horn like a rhino's sticking out of his brow was entertaining them on the didgeridoo, and eyeing up David's only remaining appendage.

Now there was someone at the door, probably offering two pizzas for the price of one. Bleary-eyed and disheveled, he opened said door to reveal Donald and Reg.

"Sorry about the time," said Donald, "but Reg and me are starving, so we thought we'd have a bacon sarnie with you – a working breakfast they call it, don't they?"

David was far too tired to offer any form of resistance. He allowed them in to the kitchen.

"So what's up this time?" he asked, preparing himself for the worst.

"Well, good news, Dave, in a nutshell. Here's your lovely wife's Rolex."

He handed David the smart green leatherette box and began

looking for the frying pan.

"Oh, fantastic!" said David, punching the air with delight. He felt more disposed to cook for them now. "Do tell all."

"Well," began Donald, "you know Dick Nibbells hadn't got a caravan?"

"Yes, so his cousin said, anyway."

"Well, his cousin was right. But guess what. He hasn't got a sister either."

"WHAT?"

"We visited him, as you suggested, and we're here now to congratulate you on helping us nail the bugger. Our boss is delighted with us, wrapping up all those burglaries in one foul sweep. I'll start from the beginning, shall I, while you get the old bacon cooking."

David did as he was told. He was at least ninety percent, if not all, ears.

"Well, first, we went to see old Barry Suggs again, and confronted him about the robberies. At the time he was supposed to be collecting his Van Gogh from Tim Beasley, he was actually at a service for his mother, who died the week before. There were about sixty witnesses, and he went round the vicarage for a cup of tea afterwards. The vicar himself can vouch for him until well after the time Tim met his client. Now don't you think it was strange that Tim insisted his client was tall, wiry and athletic, and called Barry Suggs? It perplexed us, didn't it, Reg?"

Reg nodded in agreement. It didn't take much to perplex Reg, it had to be said, but nevertheless, the two stories didn't add up.

"So then we had a word with Nibbells. We asked him to come with us to his sister's place in the High Street, as we wanted to interview them together, and then he got very flustered and kept saying he didn't know where she was. Eventually, after Reg got a bit carried away with talk of interrogation down at the nick and the like, he began to cry like a baby. And that's when he dropped the bomb. He hasn't really got a sister."

"So who is the woman that hypnotized Laz and Barry then? His lover?"

"Weirder still, mate. It's him!"

"Eh?"

"Him. Dick Nibbells has what they nowadays call a gender issue. In my day it was known as Danny la Rue. He feels, and I quote, like a woman, trapped in the body of a man. Body of a potato more like. The poor chap likes to dress as a woman a few days of the week, and the perfect solution was to become his own twin sister. It's *Dick* who is the qualified hypnotist."

David was dumbfounded. He was rarely lost for words, but now was one of those times. It was all he could do to manage turning the bacon over.

"So….."

"So Nancy was Dick and Dick was Nancy. Whenever he heard of someone at the cricket club who had a psychological problem, he'd recommend his sister. Then, dressed in female clothes, he put them under the ether and probed them, so to speak. That's how he found out about the Van Gogh, the Rolex, the Porsche, the Kawasaki, and probably loads of other things we don't know about."

"But why steal from people he knew?"

"Because the poor sod was broke, and he wanted to pay for the sex-change operation privately, somewhere abroad, where, if the colour of your money is right, they don't ask too many questions."

David looked stunned. "I should be mad with him, but I feel really sorry for him now. What an awful way to live."

"Yeah, but he stole from people, and being a trannie doesn't make you exempt from the law, Dave. We had to arrest him, old son."

Throughout their conversation, something nagged at the back of David's mind.

"But hang on. Why did everyone insist it was Barry Suggs stealing the stuff? How could Tim Beasley be fooled into thinking his client was tall and wiry, when he was built along the lines of a sumo wrestler?"

"Ah! That had us going too. Dick simply put them under, and then suggested to them that their visitor was Barry Suggs. Simple!"

"Ingenious. So the poor sod was Dick by name but not by nature, eh?"

"Yep! He wanted Dick removed, in more ways than one. I'm surprised he didn't want to be known as Fanny after the op."

David handed round the bacon sandwiches, before the tone was lowered any further. It was quite uncanny, he mused, how strange coincidences seemed to govern his life. He would remember this as the year when everyone and his dog wanted penis's removed, in one way or another.

Once breakfast was concluded and Reg was woken from his slumbers, the two coppers left David to get on with it, thanking him one more time for his intuitive detective work. He'd no sooner returned to the kitchen when the phone rang. It was a very distressed sounding Graham Gunmore-Nicholls.

"Oh, David. I'm so pleased you're in at last. I tried you fourteen times yesterday but you were out and the answering machine was off."

David gulped audibly. He feared that the game was up, and his fake had been rumbled.

"Oh, I'm, erm, sorry, Graham. I was in London. Not far from you, actually. My wife was probably out shopping, as usual. What's up?"

"A terrible, terrible thing has happened. I have smashed the Ashes urn. I tripped and dropped it, and it's completely shattered. Ruined! I have single-handedly destroyed cricket's most coveted treasure. Can you help me? I suspect the answer is no, of course."

David began to grin like the Cheshire cat. "Graham, take deep breaths, and don't reach for the arsenic just yet. You won't believe what I'm capable of. Don't do anything rash, send the bits back pronto, ring me in a couple of days and I may well have good news."

Once the distraught curator had been duly pacified, David snatched a rare moment for himself and began to peruse the newspaper. He had barely skimmed over page two when the doorbell rang again. He opened the door to find Donald and Reg, once more.

"Ah, lads!" he grinned. "Lunch isn't until one. Would you care for a martini until then?"

"Sorry, Dave," said Donald, his face tense and unsmiling. "You're under arrest, mate."

* * *

David kissed Suzanne and Lauren goodbye and told them not to worry. Lauren wasn't worried anyway, so that was good. He joined the sheepish-looking officers, who were waiting next to their patrol car. Reg opened the rear door and guided David onto the back seat, pushing his head down as he entered, just like the cops on TV always did.

"So what did I do this time?" he asked, fearing that he already knew the answer.

Donald sighed a heavy sigh. "We can't help you on this occasion, Dave. The Chief Super from the Met, no less, wants to interview you personally. He also wanted a little chat with your mate, Laz, but his missus reckons he's had to go to Plymouth early this morning to sort out problems with a steak house that he's refurbishing. Never mind, we'll catch up with him eventually. Meanwhile, we have to drive you to London to face the music on your own. The Chief rang me a few minutes ago, and I couldn't believe what he had to say."

"Go on. I can't flipping wait."

"He said that he went to scatter his father's ashes over the Lord's ground yesterday, so it was a bit of a sad morning. Afterwards, he decided to get a coffee in a small café by the ground, and he was in the loo, minding his own business, so to speak, when three tubs of Strawberry ice-cream were thrown into the cubicle. Ring any bells so far?"

David groaned. "Raspberry ripple, actually."

"So it *was* you!"

"Go on."

"Well, one bounced off his head and the other two missed him, and he's thinking, 'why's someone throwing ice cream about.'"

"You would, wouldn't you?"

"Anyway, he belts out of the bog after this chap with a pigtail. There can't be many folks nowadays with one of them, can there?"

"No."

"And he loses the chap after he sent half a ton of mixed fruit and veg cascading across the pavement. Now, being the Chief Super, and a very thorough chap, he decides to re-visit the caff looking for clues, and guess what he finds? The waitress says that two men, one matching the pigtail's description, paid by cheque, and surprise surprise! The cheque was signed by one David Day esquire. Well, it's a bloody small world, eh?"

David sank into his seat and closed his eyes. Alarm bells were ringing, and they weren't the tinny little irritating ones that upset Laz each morning. They were huge, deafening brass ones, as used by Quasimodo during his stint at Notre Dame.

"But the story doesn't end there, Dave. As if the poor bloke wasn't having a bad enough day, he got home to find he'd been burgled, and guess what the thieves stole? Go on, guess?"

"His truncheon?"

"No. They stole his beloved pet dog's ashes. He's out at Lord's, scattering his dad's ashes, and meanwhile, someone's at his house stealing his dog's ashes. Whoever said truth is stranger than fiction knew what he was on about. That wouldn't be anything to do with you, would it, Dave?"

David became overwhelmed with an awful feeling of nausea. All of a sudden, everything was becoming clear, but having briefly experienced clarity, he began to prefer the pea-soup fog whence he was slowly emerging. He closed his eyes, sank back into his chair, and remained that way until they arrived at New Scotland Yard.

* * *

"Ah! David, do come in," said Chief Superintendent Trilby cordially. He gestured for his guest to sit, and David did as he was told.

"I'm very well, thank you," said David nervously.

"I didn't ask," replied the policeman, a touch frostily, David thought.

Donald and Reg were also asked to sit down, once the Chief Super's speed-walking sycophant had returned with more chairs.

"Well," continued the Superintendent, "you certainly are an enigma, aren't you, David? No – shush - no need to answer at this point, just listen for the time being, please. Had we conducted this little interview yesterday, I fear I would not have been rational. Luckily for you, I've calmed down a bit today, so why don't you explain to me, in your own time, what, if anything, is going on in your head?"

David realized that the game was up, and his only course of action now was to tell the truth, the whole truth and nothing but the truth, in the hope that his sentence would be commuted to life imprisonment.

"How long have we got?" he asked nervously.

"As long as it takes."

"I'll start at the beginning then, omitting no detail, however slight. When I first came to see you, it was to warn you that I'd overheard a conversation in a lavatory between two Australians. They were planning to steal the Ashes to order, or so I was led to believe, for a man named Maurice J. Trilby."

At this, the Chief Super's facial expression changed, like a dog's does when he hears his dinner bowl being rattled.

"So I walk into your office and spot that you are called M. J. Trilby, which throws me somewhat."

"It would. Do go on, I'm fascinated now."

"The chances of having two Australian M. J. Trilbys were a million to one, I thought. That shows what a good gambler I am, I suppose. I now realize, thanks to my two friends here, that you are Michael, not Maurice. So, believing you to be Maurice, whoever he is, I make up a real cock and bull story about a gang of art

146

thieves, because it was the best thing I could come up with at very short notice."

"It did sound ridiculous."

"Obviously, I couldn't confide in you, so I decided to thwart your plans and rescue the Ashes myself, with Laz's help – that's the chap with the pigtail."

"Bless him! How is he?"

"Excellent. He couldn't join us today, as he's busy in Plymouth, trying to rectify a problem on site. The fitters have put his stripy carpet in a bar with the stripes going in the wrong direction."

"It happens."

"Anyway, I digress."

"You do, prithee continue."

"So Laz and I mistakenly assumed that you were a bent policeman – and I see now that this was nonsense, of course – so we decided to stand guard at the ground, waiting for the two Aussies to show up at four-thirty. That was what they wrote on their map."

Chief Superintendent Trilby ruffled his hair the way Stan Laurel used to do. He was being taken into dark and uncharted waters now.

"What map?"

"Well, the two Aussies played cricket at Enville, near my house, as part of their English tour, and afterwards they got plastered and ended up at Laz's house, where he allowed them to sleep it off. Laz is a bit more of a party animal than me, you see. He's what you'd call gregarious."

"It's not what I'd call him."

"No. So when Laz wakes up, the two have scarpered with his

fifty quid, and Laz finds a map of what I thought was the Lord's trophy room or something, saying that the alarm would be off at four-thirty. I presume I'm right in thinking that this was a map of your house."

"Correct. So do these charmers have a name?"

David's face lit up. He loved helping the police with their enquiries - it was fun. "Yes, Mervin and Brett. I heard them call each other by their names when they were in the lavatory, plotting. I did say plotting by the way, not plopping." David seemed extremely amused with his own, puerile joke.

The Chief Super sat bolt upright in his chair on hearing this latest news. He seemed to be warming to David now, which was good.

"Mervin Dudley and Brett Snipes. Well I never. It has to be them; there can't be two sets of Australian Mervins and Bretts, surely."

"Don't involve me in that kind of speculation, sir," replied David with feeling. "My track record is not good."

"Granted. It is a coincidence though. Describe them for me, if you can."

"One's scraggy looking, unshaven with blond hair. The other's scraggy looking, unshaven, with blond hair."

"That's them. They work for my brother back in Sydney. My brother, by the way, is named Maurice Trilby, just to put your mind at ease. I think it's fair to say we don't get on. In fact, he's the black sheep of the family, and these two lowlifes do his dirty work for him. That's breaking and entering, burglary and stealing fifty quid for a start. Good! I presume Maurice sent them to steal my father's ashes. Thank goodness they arrived too late for that, but they did take something of mine and I want it back. Where are they now, do you think?"

148

David said that he didn't know, but was willing to speculate.

"Where would any unemployed Australian be today? The test match, I'd have thought. I did hear them say they'd be heading home once they stolen the Ashes though, so I wouldn't imagine they'd be hanging around too long after the game."

"Nor would I. I think I'll get a few of the boys to check the exits and entrances today, and see if we can pick these jokers up. Maurice has always managed to avoid getting arrested, but I could have something on him here that would send him away, and, churlish as it sounds, considering that he's flesh and blood, it couldn't happen to a nicer bloke."

Donald, who had been silently observing David and Michael's coming together of minds, finally piped up.

"Excuse me, sir. I told you didn't I? He might seem dodgy, but there's always a logical reason for David's weird behaviour."

Reg would have endorsed this, had he not been taking a nap. The Chief Super had to admit that he felt less inclined to throttle David, now that he was cognizant of the facts. He added, however, that he'd still like to give Laz a good kicking, just for the hell of it. Instead, he settled for a slightly sanctimonious sermon.

"Well, David, I can see that you were acting in what you presumed were the best interests of the country, but in future, you should trust the integrity of the police. If I have a problem, I confront people square on, not make up a tissue of preposterous lies."

"What, so you really do play golf with me then?"

"Yes, well…."

"And do you still want me to restore your Constable, now this is all sorted out?"

"I, erm - look, okay, thirty-love. Now is there anything else I should know about? Any gangs of art thieves on the loose?"

149

"No, I think that's about the size of it."

"Good. Well let's shake hands and call it quits. Thank you for bringing David in today, officer. You and Rip Van Winkle can take our artist home now, and I'll get some lads over to the ground with a description of Mervin and Brett."

The three men were headed for the door, when Chief Superintendent Trilby called David.

"Oh, just one last thing. It's been playing on my mind, you see. Why ice-cream, in the name of God?"

"Ah," frowned David, "We, erm, saw it in a comedy film once, and it kind of stuck in our minds. They used it to sort-of cause a distraction."

Trilby shook his head sadly, the way one would upon discovering that one's twelve-year-old son has inadvertently set fire to one's potting shed.

"But this isn't a comedy film, David. This is real life. Try and discern the difference, is my advice to you."

And with that, he bade them 'G'day!'

Chapter 16

A Tissue of Lies

David was listening to the test match on the radio as he restored the urn, just to put him in the right frame of mind. As predicted, England were getting caned, just as they had been in the first test at Old Trafford. Day One had ended with Australia on two-hundred and ninety-two for two, and now it was five-hundred and ninety-two for four at close of play. Bleary-eyed from his exacting and precise work, he turned off his table lamp and turned in. He was about to vacate his Fortress of Solitude in favour of the barn's cosy living room and a glass of red, when the phone rang. It was the fretful and now borderline suicidal Graham Gunmore-Nicholls. David had been looking forward to this promised phone call all day, and here it was.

"David, you said I should ring this evening, and you'd have a clearer picture. I've had to lie through my teeth about where the urn had gone, blaming restoration problems and so on. We've had hundreds of bitterly disappointed visitors who've had to make do with the replica. Can you help me? I presume not, as the ten thousand pieces I sent you look completely beyond repair, to my untrained eye, at any rate."

David loved giving good news. He was very altruistic in that respect. He took a deep breath and launched into it.

"Graham. Put the aspirin back in the medicine chest, and cancel that order for the pack of cut-throat razors. I am your saviour. Yesterday, I was talking to the Chief Superintendent of the Metropolitan police – we play golf together - so I am now in a position to inform you of a little bit of subterfuge that's been going on, and I'm only sorry I couldn't disclose any of this earlier. A gang of Australians, posing as cricketers, were planning to steal the Ashes from the Lord's trophy room, and the Chief Super, or Mike, as I call him, got wind of it. Then - and this must surely be the most fortuitous and coincidental situation of the century - you sent me the Ashes to restore. I'd told no one they were at my studio, as you and I agreed, but I admit that did mention it to Mike as we played a round of golf together. I only confided in him because I knew I could trust him, of course, and I could guarantee it wouldn't go any further. Well, when he told me he was a cricket buff, he'd arranged to meet you, and he was planning to scatter his father's ashes at the ground, you could have knocked me down with a feather. All of a sudden, upon hearing my news, his face went ashen, if you'll excuse the pun, and he said that my sharing this confidence couldn't have come at a more opportune time, as he'd unearthed this plot. He asked me to keep hold of the original urn, and create a bogus one, so that, if the Aussies slipped through the net, they wouldn't be getting away with the real McCoy. I asked Mike if I should tell you – keep you in the loop, sort of thing – and he ordered me, quite categorically, not to tell *anyone*. He couldn't risk anything leaking out, you see. I know we're mates and everything, but when Mike says jump, you jump. He's that kind of bloke is Mike, so I did what I was told. To cut a long story short, and some would argue it's already too late for that, his officers arrested the would-be thieves before they could carry out their plan, and now I can put your troubled mind at rest. The real Ashes are restored and awaiting pick-up. Once the Securigard boys arrive, and I've signed there, there and there, they're all yours! That's four consecutive 'theres' in one sentence, by the way! Anyway, I'm just sorry I couldn't confide in you when you were in a state the other day."

This lengthy diatribe was met with a stony silence. David enquired as to the other's health, fearing that he had swooned or even passed away, and this seemed to do the trick. David's direct question had acted in a similar way to the electric paddles that surgeons often use, in order to shock the patient's heart into beating again.

"Oh gosh!" spluttered the museum curator, for he was not one to utter profanities. "I'm sorry, David, it's hard for me to take it all in. So you're saying that the real urn isn't broken."

"Correct!"

"And you have it safe at your studio?"

"Yep!"

"David, I am not a homosexual."

"I'm not sure how to respond to that, actually."

"But if I were, I would kiss you."

"Steady on."

"In fact, I may just do that regardless."

"Not necessary. I'm just pleased for you, and I can only apologize for the deceit. I was under orders."

"I understand. I'll send the armoured car first thing tomorrow. And can you do me one last, huge favour please?"

"Name it."

"When the security firm comes for the urn, could you please check to see if whatever box you send it in is free of eight-legged inhabitants before you wrap it? I have to confess that I suffer from arachnophobia, and it was the sight of one of those horrible creatures within the old mahogany box that caused me to jump and drop the urn. Please don't laugh at me. I know it's irrational, but one can't help one's phobias."

David assured Mr Gunmore-Nicholls that he would check the box thoroughly before packing the urn, and was on the verge of recommending a hypnotist when thankfully, Suzanne called him to say that his dinner was ready.

After the family had eaten, David sat at the dining room table with Lauren, trying to show her how to draw a princess, a shark and a teddy bear, in the order named. Her teacher seemed to think that she had inherited some of her father's talent, and she could even identify the styles of the various famous fine artists that they had discussed in class. Keen to put this to the test, David showed her a reproduction of Van Gogh's sunflowers in one of his many art books and asked her to guess who had painted it. To his surprise, and immense satisfaction, she guessed correctly.

"He cut his ear off," she informed him in a matter-of-fact way, pointing to another reproduction in the book, showing a heavily-bandaged self portrait. "Mrs Staples told us."

"Why do you think he did that?" asked David, wondering why his teacher had seen fit to give them all the gory details.

"Because he wanted to draw round it!" explained Lauren. "And did you know, Daddy, that Leonardo di Caprio invented the helicopter?"

The art lesson was interrupted by the front doorbell, followed by a five minute discussion between David and Suzanne about who the unknown caller could possibly be. Once double-glazing salesmen, Jehovah's Witnesses and political canvassers had been ruled out on the grounds that they always called halfway through dinner, but rarely after it, that just left any of David and Suzanne's combined friends, parents or possibly Donald and Reg. Eventually, they jointly decided that the best way to find out was to actually take a look, and hope that the caller hadn't died of old age in the meantime. Suzanne peeked through the gap in the curtains, but did not know the man. She invited David to take a look, and after a second or two, he announced that it was none other than Barry Suggs, whereupon he finally opened the door and said hello.

"I didn't recognize you with that beard," smiled David. "Come on in."

"I didn't *have* a beard when I first rang the doorbell," replied Barry, somewhat sarcastically. He wiped his feet and entered.

"I won't stop," he said, "but I just wanted to say thank you. The two policemen told me that you'd stuck up for me and said all along that you didn't think I was the culprit. I must say though, it was a hell of a shock being accused of stealing all that stuff."

"It must have been," replied David. "There's one thing that I still don't get though, and what with all the excitement, I forgot to ask the police when they came. Why did Dick Nibbells try to put the blame on you?"

Barry reddened a little. "Ah, good question. It turns out that he, erm, fancied me. Stop laughing please. He wasn't a homosexual – not in the true sense, because he thought he was a woman. I met Nancy Nibbells at one of the cricket club dances and she was all over me, asking me to dance and whatnot. Eventually I had to tell her quite forcefully that she wasn't my type, and besides, I was engaged to be married. I've never been drawn to fat, female pygmies. I shudder to think what would have happened if I *had* fancied her and offered to take her home on my motorbike afterwards. One Dick is fine, but three's a crowd in my book, if you follow me. It's quite funny, looking back. I asked her where her brother was, and she said he'd had to go away on business, so he'd given her his ticket. I should have suspected there and then, because Dick's never had any business to be away on. Anyway, he, or she, must have harboured a grudge after that night, so I got set up for all the robberies. Hell hath no fury like a woman scorned, eh? And yet, she seemed sociable enough when I had to turn to her for my wasp treatment."

David thought about this. "Yeah, but maybe she was secretly

thrilled that the object of her affections was at last under her control. I'll bet she spent ten minutes working on your wasp problem and the rest of the hour trying to get you to fancy her – or worse, she may have got physical!"

Barry blanched at the prospect. "Good God! I never thought about that. I don't think I could fancy her, even if I was hypnotized, but I must admit, I've started to find Jim, our wicket keeper attractive lately."

"I hope that was a joke," smiled David.

"Of course it was," laughed Barry, before turning away and biting his knuckle.

The doorbell rang again, and Suzanne went off to answer it, re-entering seconds later with Laz, who'd popped around to enquire as to his current standing vis-à-vis the Metropolitan police. He greeted Barry warmly, congratulating him on his early release, and spread himself across David's vacant leather settee. Not wishing to disrupt David's busy social life, Barry stood up and headed for the door.

"Oh, and there aren't loads more Enville third team games this season, Dave," he said, "and you still haven't knocked anywhere near fifty!"

"Gee, thanks for reminding him," groaned David, "but at least, with his hypnotist out of the equation, Laz won't be able to pack in smoking either, so it won't matter."

"Don't kid yourself," piped up Laz, "the bet's still on, my son, and we haven't agreed a forfeit yet either, by the way."

"Well now's the perfect time to do so, in the presence of witnesses," replied David. "Lauren, can Daddy borrow some drawing paper please?"

"No."

"Oh, okay, wait a bit; I'll get a couple of my letterheads and an envelope. Right, Laz. You write on there what you want me to do if I don't knock fifty in a bona-fide Enville game before the end of the season, and I'll write on this one what you have to do if you haven't completely, and I mean completely, given up the weed. Agreed?"

"Agreed. Barry, you witness this and take the sealed envelope away with you, to be opened at the end of season barbecue."

David and Laz sat at either end of David's kitchen table, writing out their forfeits, their hands cupped over their work so that the other couldn't copy, like ten-year-olds in an exam. Laz's tongue poked out at a jaunty angle as his pen scratched away furiously, whilst David preferred to stare for long periods at the ceiling in between words, as if digging deep for inspiration. Eventually, after Barry had told them to stop writing and hand in their work, the papers were folded and inserted into the envelope, which their adjudicator promptly consigned to his inside jacket pocket. Then, all that remained was to open the bottle of red and consummate the deal.

* * *

The following morning, bright and early, the Securigard men were at the door once again to collect the troublesome little urn, so that they could return it to the safety of its nice mahogany box. David blasted the inside of the packing box with compressed air from his airbrush hose to remove any wayward insects, and piously laid the relic into its concave bubble-wrap bed. Hopefully, this was the last he would see of it for a while.

As soon as he closed the door, the studio phone began to ring. Henry Tibbatts was in a state.

"David, I have awful news," he began. "Just before we closed for the day, some bloody madman suddenly attacked your restored

157

Van Gogh with a fork that he'd purloined from our café. According to security, he screamed 'die, die, die, you one-eared bastard', and slashed at it about twenty times. I'm afraid it is utterly beyond repair. Ruined! Is there anything we can do? I'm desperate."

David's smirk was in danger of exceeding the legal limit. He composed himself as best he could, and returned the telephone to his mouth.

"Henry, Henry, calm down. I have some very good news for you. You know I'm big friends with the Chief Super from the Met. Yes, Mike, that's right, we play golf together. Well, recently, he confided in me, as he often does, about a gang of art thieves, called the Black Penis Gang. Have you ever come across them?"

"No, but Superintendent Trilby actually asked me about that very group, quite recently."

"Oh, did he now? Well apparently, these people recruit unstable types and pay them peanuts to deface great works of art: the name of the gang was derived from their practice of adding black, felt-pen penis cartoons to the paintings."

"Good God! Our Van Gogh!"

"Exactly, and then, of course, the galleries have to employ a restorer to remove said appendage. This gang somehow finds out who is restoring the painting, and then steals the picture while it is in transit, often from the security vans. It's fiendishly clever, don't you think? Mike asked me if I'd heard of them, and I said no, but coincidentally, I was actually in the process of restoring that painting at the time. He informed me that my studio could be at risk, and posted plain-clothed detectives all over the place. I asked Mike if I could warn you about it, but he said he was in the middle of an undercover mission to catch the gang, and it was better if no-one at all knew what was happening. He also got me to fake the Van Gogh, so that, if the gang did get away with it, it was worthless. The good news is, Mike finally arrested the lot of them at an address in, erm, Wandsworth, and the threat is over."

"Well, that's incredible. I can scarcely believe it! Your fake was utterly convincing, I'm embarrassed to say. So you still have my real Van Gogh?"

"Absolutely, and I was about to phone you to announce the good news, now that Mike had given me permission to, when you rang me."

Henry was a very happy fellow, but something was still exercising him.

"So who was this bloke who hacked the fake Van Gogh to pieces with a fork?"

"Lord knows. A genuine nutter, I presume. You'll still be plagued with them, unfortunately. He wasn't one of the gang's pet nutters though, that's for sure. He set out to completely wreck the picture, whereas your Black Penis foot soldiers only ever added marks that a restorer could remove easily."

"Well, I'm blowed."

"Don't be. Just pour yourself a gin and tonic, ring the Securigard people, and tell them to fetch the Van Gogh first thing tomorrow."

"David, I don't know what to say. I am so grateful to you and the Chief Super. I may well ring him to offer my congratulations."

"Erm, don't! He's, erm, on holiday in Australia at the moment."

Henry tapped his brow twice with the palm of his hand. "Of course he is. He's bringing back that oil painting for you to restore isn't he? Apparently, he may have been left a Constable with an umbrella hole in it."

David removed the receiver from his ear and gawped at it. There were so many complete lies floating around now that he'd lost count, and it was bound to end in tears.

"Oh, there goes the doorbell again," he said, panicking. "Must fly."

He quickly replaced the receiver and stood pondering awhile. Having lied through his teeth about the doorbell, it came as a huge shock when the bell actually rang, seconds later. David opened the door to find Donald and Reg. Donald was holding a parcel.

"Thrice hello!" smiled the officer, and handed the parcel to David.

"Your Van Gogh returned, sir," added Reg. "Any tea on the go?"

David invited them in and unwrapped the parcel. It was his Tim Beasley model. Sometimes it was difficult to remember with three floating around.

"We forgot to bring it round the other day with your wife's Rolex. Sorry, mate."

"Thank you," said David, "I'll put it with the other one."

Donald and Reg removed their headwear and made themselves at home, whilst David attended to the breakfasts.

"The Chief Super sends his regards," said Donald, "and wanted me to pass on some news. He sent a handful of constables to Lord's, as he told you he would, and caught himself two jolly Australian swagmen."

"Oh, great news! Were they camped by a billabong, under the shade of a Kulabar tree by any chance?"

"No, they were spark-out next to a public bar with cans of Fosters strewn all around. The officers waltzed them off for a chat with Trilby, and he's done them for breaking and entering, the theft of his pet dog's ashes, nicking fifty quid from your mate, and around forty other crimes they asked to be taken into consideration. They also sang like canaries about his brother, Maurice, and his many illegal activities back in Oz, which pleased

160

him no-end. No love lost there, I'm afraid. He said to pass on his thanks for helping nail them, but also added a word of caution about your tendency to tell tall tales. It all worked out okay on this occasion, but he warned us that if he heard of any more bizarre goings on that could be directly attributed to you, he wouldn't be as easy going the next time. In other words, always tell the bloody police, Dave. That's what we're there for."

"Okay, point taken. Do you like the rind cut off, Reg?"

"Yes please."

"And what about poor old Dick Nibbells? What will his fate be?"

Donald smiled a sad smile and sipped at his tea.

"I think they'll go easy on him. I hope they do anyway. It can't be any fun being trapped in the wrong body, can it?"

"I don't know. Ask Laz."

"That's different," replied Donald. "That's the right *type* of body. He just ordered one two sizes too big, that's all. I reckon Dick will be out in a few months, maximum."

"Yeah! He'll probably hypnotize the warden into suggesting he gets early release. Either that or they'll end up getting married."

The three men ate their bacon sandwiches in reverential silence, and then the two officers replaced their hats, thanked David for his hospitality and set about their daily grind. David, too, had a busy day planned. He had to remove a crudely painted nineteenth century addition to an eighteenth century seascape and restore it to its original condition. It was, by his standards, a boring task, so he poured himself another tea and began to listen to the test commentary on the radio. It was not going England's way. Australia had declared on six-hundred and thirty-two for four, and now it was England's turn. David winced as he heard the latest score, but had to allow himself a wry smile, knowing that,

161

whatever happened, the Ashes would remain at Lord's. On the face of it, the Australians didn't seem to have been handed a great deal. The two teams played for the Ashes, and usually Australia won, but for some reason, the urn remained in an English museum. It was a little like saying, "We'll play cards for this ten pound note, and if you win, we'll agree that it's yours, but I'll keep it in my wallet, just to make sure it's safe." Whoever sold the Aussies that one, David reasoned, would make a great double-glazing rep.

It was just after Graeme Hick strode to the crease uttering a silent prayer that the studio doorbell rang for the umpteenth time that week. The Securigard lads were back yet again, this time to collect the Van Gogh. Just lately, they seemed to be infesting the place, and their van was beginning to wear deep grooves in David's gravel drive.

He fetched the Van Gogh and completed the necessary paperwork, which always necessitated the signing of at least three signatures and a vague guess at the time of day before his visitors declared themselves satisfied. As they clumped down the studio steps, David called after them to wait a second, and handed them the other Van Gogh, just in case Henry needed a spare. This seemed to take the two men into deep and uncharted waters, as they had no paperwork to deal with it. There was much scratching of helmets and tut-tutting, but eventually, David persuaded them that it was his occasional 'buy one, get one free offer', and this seemed to pacify them a little.

Chapter 17

A Glorious Summer of Cricket

England lost convincingly in the second test, by an innings and sixty-two runs, and new boy, Warne, continued to spin his way into the record books at their expense.

Graham Gunmore-Nicholls had kindly sent David an envelope stuffed with free tickets for the remaining games, as a gesture of thanks, which meant that he and Laz were able to follow the national team around the country for one, glorious summer, giving the two old friends the opportunity to see their heroes get trounced up north, just as they had been down south. Trent Bridge saw England scrape a draw, but at Headingley, they reverted to their losing ways, and continued the trend at David's home ground, Edgbaston. Finally, however, things came right for them at the Oval, and they won the sixth test fairly convincingly. It was the first one they'd managed to win against their arch rivals since Melbourne in nineteen-eighty-six, and it just about prevented them from committing mass hara-kiri with the sharp end of the cricket stumps in front of their down-trodden fans.

David and Laz were philosophical though, for despite the fact that results had not gone their way, they had been treated to a wonderful spectacle, and for a few, mad weeks, they had themselves become part of cricketing history. Laz would be able to dine out for years to come on his tale of how he and his best

163

friend had prevented the Ashes from falling into enemy hands. Careful scrutiny would have revealed that the actual Ashes were never in any danger from the Australian thieves, and all Laz had in fact prevented was the dumping of an incinerated German Shepherd into Sydney Harbour. Laz, however, wasn't one to let the truth stand in the way of a good story, and besides, David *had* been asked to restore the sacred urn, so it all sort-of fitted together. By the time he'd retold the saga ten times, the crooks would have had machine guns and he would have personally taken on at least five burly thugs in the Long Room, armed only with a Duncan Fearnley bat and a cork ball.

In sharp contrast to the fortunes of the national side, the Canberra Convicts' tour of England was not a resounding success. After playing twenty games at clubs the length and breadth of England, the latter ones without Mervin and Brett, they had managed one win and one draw, and the win was less than ethical, to say the least. A game had been arranged against the inmates of a North London centre that specialized in treating alcoholism and drug dependency. Its patients were mainly unemployed, or with only modest incomes, unlike the Betty Ford Clinic or the Priory, where the celebrity drunks preferred to go, so there were no disgraced professional sportsmen to bolster up the cricket team. That said, the clinic had managed to put together a half-decent outfit, which had performed reasonably well against the local league teams. Realizing that they were almost certainly due for yet another thrashing, certain team members had taken it upon themselves to spike the home team's lemonades with vodka, which seemed to rapidly revitalize their latent interest in all things alcoholic. Intent on making up for lost time, virtually all of the St. Saviours' Centre Eleven, with the notable exception of Jacko McGiven and Paddy Johnson, developed huge thirsts during the tea interval, and were rendered mentally and physically incapable just in time for their turn with the bat. Jacko and Paddy liked a drink, but decided to jump ship in search of something a little stronger, and arrived back at the centre completely out of their minds on crack cocaine, seconds after the Convicts had narrowly recorded their maiden victory against a stupefied opposition. By this time, the centre's staff had put two and two together, ended up with four, and were intent on having deep and meaningful dialogue with their antipodean cousins. Never ones to outstay their welcome, the Australians saw this as an opportune time to head for the tour bus and explore pastures new, sadly bereft of their first-ever sporting trophy.

Having examined the fortunes of the teams operating at the extreme ends of the cricket spectrum, it now seems an opportune time to reflect on Enville. By their standards, the season had been reasonably satisfactory, in that they were neither grubbing around at the bottom of the league table, nor flying high and challenging for promotion at the top. No one had caned their backsides, there had been no ignominious humiliations, and nor had they handed out any to visiting sides. Things were nice and steady, and that's how they liked it. Barry Suggs had finally put his unfortunate few weeks in June behind him and gone on to knock a decent few runs, take a couple of wickets and hang onto a handful of catches.

David too, had not done too badly, considering. He'd played regularly in the third team, and managed thirty-five against Netherton, his best so far. With only one league game left, however, he would have to pull something spectacular out of the bag in order to win his bet. Laz was still puffing away at his cigarettes with gay abandon though, which did reduce the pressure somewhat, coupled with the fact that Ridgwood Cricket Club, David's final opponents, were notoriously hopeless at bowling. If scoring fifty was possible at all, Saturday's game was a good bet, and if all else failed, there was the end of season barbecue after the game. He could always drown his sorrows in alcohol.

It had been a quite magical summer, all told, and after a frenetic June, life had begun to slow down. There had been no more incidents of note, no paintings defaced by genitalia, no visits from Donald and Reg, no panic calls from Graham Gunmore-Nicholls, no sign of Tim Beasley, and Chief Superintendent Trilby had disappeared off the radar. This was how David liked it, but he knew it probably wouldn't last. It never had done, not in forty years.

This was the lull before the storm.

The first sign of bad weather came on the Monday morning, when David examined his answering machine messages from the weekend. The first one was from a man called Eric, who wanted to know how much David would charge him to paint his dog. Eric did not have any good photos of the animal, which had unfortunately expired the previous Wednesday. David reluctantly returned the call, but was met with another answering machine. He informed Eric, via the machine, that he could give the animal two coats of emulsion for ten quid. He didn't think Eric would bother to ring again.

The next message chilled David's blood. It was Trilby. He'd been away in Australia, assisting the Sydney Police with a big trial. His brother, Maurice Trilby, was looking at a long stretch for tax evasion, running a brothel, drug-dealing and parking on a disabled space, and Michael was there to add a few extra crimes to the list, just in case. His duty done, he was now back, and desirous of a word. He seemed particularly interested in discussing the Black Penis Gang, the faked Ashes and David's golfing handicap. Wiping his messages, David began to chew his nails furiously. Maybe, he reasoned, if he ignored it, it would go away, but just in case it didn't he began to ponder a few alternative explanations.

Luckily, he was not able to give Trilby's call much space in his head, due to a rather oppressive work-load. Henry Tibbatts had sent him a Cubist period Picasso with a large dull patch near the centre, which he had now treated, and as soon as that was safely handed over to the couriers, there was a nice little David Cox watercolour that needed work.

The couriers appeared at the appointed time, and produced the usual paperwork. At least, David presumed it was the usual paperwork – he'd have signed gas bills, confessions or death warrants at that time of the morning, and not noticed. What he did manage to notice was the lady courier. Usually, it was two men, but this day it was a lady and a dumpy-looking character with a preposterous folk singer's beard. Beardy, who looked sullen, hung around halfway up the steps looking sheepish, leaving the female to do all the work. She was a striking creature, but not in the same way that, say, Lauren Bacall was striking. This woman was more akin to Lee Marvin, if anything. The crash helmet was covering up virtually all of her hairdo, but David just knew instinctively that it would be cropped short, in a skinhead style. She was devoid of all make-up, which was a pity, because she was in dire need of some, and her fingers were tobacco-stained, with chewed nails. Both hands revealed evidence of home-made tattoos that appeared to have been done whilst still at junior school, judging by the spelling, and her breath was a mixture of Park Drive and Labrador.

"Alright, mate?" she asked, with all the femininity of a council estate bricklayer. "You need to sign these and hand over a paintin'."

Beardy appeared completely uninterested, and couldn't even bother to face the right way. David signed and disappeared back inside his studio, emerging a few seconds later with the boxed Picasso. Lee Marvin grabbed it and mumbled, "Cheers! See ya!" and swaggered down the stairs with Beardy in tow. As she crossed the courtyard to the van, David could hear her whistling a jaunty tune. He walked back into his studio, shuddering visibly. It was bad enough having couriers traipsing up and down his steps every five minutes or so, but at least most of them were halfway civil, on a good day, if not exactly scintillating company. He'd never clapped eyes on this female one before, but he hoped she was a one-off, who was merely standing in for the regular couriers while they were on holiday or at their great granny's funeral. She was obviously a few chromosomes short of the required amount – or was it too many? He could never remember - and as for old Beardy, he would be well advised to pop out to the summer sales and get himself a personality while they were half price.

David was cleaning his drawing board and getting ready to begin a small job for Birmingham Art Gallery when the studio doorbell rang once more. With his trademark heavy sigh, he opened the door to greet the Keystone Cops.

"Ah, lads," he smiled, "I've missed you. Come in."

Donald and Reg headed for the comfy chesterfield, while David instinctively headed for the frying pan.

"To what do I owe the pleasure? Has Chief Superintendent Trilby sent you to arrest me again?"

"No, Dave. Have you been doing anything to cause him to arrest you?"

"Erm, not as such. So what's up?"

"We have news of Dick Nibbells. He's escaped."

"What?"

"Escaped. We thought we'd better tell you in case he pokes his nose around here. It was thanks to your detective skills that we nailed him, so he might just be harbouring a grudge and come after you with a carving knife or machete."

"Oh right. I love how you lads always put me at ease. Marvellous! How would he know that I was anything to do with his arrest anyway?"

"Oh," said Reg, "that was probably my fault. I mentioned to him that it was you who'd put two and two together about the robberies the day we nailed him."

"Cheers!"

"Well, we had to give you due credit. If we'd pretended that we'd worked it all out by ourselves, you'd have accused us of stealing the limelight. We can't do right for doing wrong sometimes, us policemen."

David groaned. He tried to articulate his feelings, which were, as usual, many and varied, but didn't know where to start. Eventually, with a gargantuan effort, he managed the inevitable question.

"So how did he escape then? Did you accidentally leave him the keys to his cell to play with?"

"No, though we have actually done that once, haven't we Donald? No, what happened was, Nibbells was due in court, and he was being taken there by a couple of security guards – a bloke and a woman. They stop off at a service station near Brum so as the bloke can have a piss, and then the woman guard just drove off with Nibbells, leaving her colleague bloody stranded: they haven't been seen since. Turns out they'd got a bit of a thing going on between them. She'd had to pick him up before for another court appearance, and got chatting to him, so the other guard says. He reckons they were getting a bit too pally for his liking, but didn't think any more of it. He'd left 'em chatting at the court for half an hour, while he popped out for a fag, and come back to find her hanging on his every word. Now he's really in the shit for losing his van, his prisoner and his partner in the two minutes it took to have a piss, buy a pork pie and a copy of Esquire magazine. Strikes me, he hypnotized her."

"Maybe he did. It's all a bit odd," said David, his brow furrowed with thought. "Dick wasn't technically a homosexual, he just fancied Barry because he believed himself to be a woman, so how come he's fallen for this security guard lady?"

"Good question, Dave. This security guard isn't your average woman. She's, well, a dyke. Her colleague – the chap who was having a piss - said she acted more like a bloke than a woman. A Martha who wants to be an Arthur, kind of thing, so maybe Dick fancied her because he *thinks* he's a woman, and she thinks she's a bloke.

"So, hang on a bit," said Donald, scratching his head. "At the moment then, he's reverted to being a heterosexual, because he now fancies this woman, right?"

"Right," confirmed Reg. "But as soon as he gets the chop, he'll temporarily become a lesbian."

"Got you, and then, if *she* gets a sex change and becomes a man, they'll both be heterosexual again, but swapped around."

"Correct."

David was no longer following this discussion. He'd gone very quiet and he was trying hard to stop his spindly legs from buckling. A bead of sweat trickled down his brow, and he raised his hand, as an eleven-year-old boy in a classroom would do when he needed the toilet.

"Lads. Shut up a minute. They've just been here. I've seen them."

"Who?"

"Dick Nibbells and Lee Marvin."

Donald seemed puzzled. "What? The guitarist in the Shadows?"

"That's Hank Marvin, cretin. Two security guards just came for a Picasso painting. I was expecting them, so there was no reason to be concerned about that. She - and I use the term loosely - did all the talking and got me to sign the forms. He just kind of held back and looked sheepish. He was a small, dumpy thing with a beard – looked just like a garden gnome. I bet he got that beard from Kettle's joke shop. It looked totally artificial, come to think of it."

Donald stroked his chin. "This painting. Was it worth a lot of money?"

"It was a Picasso."

"Yes, you said, but was it worth a lot of money?"

David stared at his ceiling. "Yes. A few million quid, probably."

"HOW MUCH?"

"You heard me. Most of the stuff that comes through here is worth loads of money."

"Bloody hell!"

"Bloody hell is about right. And I am not getting my paints out again. I've had enough."

"Christ, Dave!" exclaimed Reg. "Which way did their van turn when it left your barn?"

"Left. That narrows it down a bit eh? You'd better go left and see if you can find them. Meanwhile, if you'll excuse me, I'm going to put my finger in that light socket over there and end it all."

* * *

David had calmed down sufficiently to realize that the light socket option wasn't the best way forward. In fact, it would probably have been the best way backward, if his last major electric shock had been anything to go by. He'd picked up his Les Paul guitar a few years previously with the intention of playing along to 'All Right Now' on the radio. He could remember switching on his Marshall amplifier and striking the chord of A Major, but after that it all became a blur. Somehow he'd been catapulted ten feet backwards, slammed into a wall at the other end of the room and inherited a dislocated arm and six string burns across his face. He did recollect the pain though, which was roughly equivalent to twelve Irish navvies hitting him with sledge-

171

hammers in the deep end of the swimming baths. He remembered lying on the ground and calmly announcing to himself that he was about to die, as his brains boiled inside his head, and after that, nothing. Until, that was, Suzanne asked him if he was okay at the hospital, at which point he remembered crying his eyes out and shaking violently.

No, the light socket comment had been a joke. Anyone who has suffered one big shock doesn't deliberately seek out the next one. What he *really* needed was a change of scenery in a hurry, preferably in conjunction with vigorous exercise, so that he hadn't got time to brood over things. It was the day before the final cricket match of the season. Perhaps it would do him good to spend an hour in the nets. He hastily gathered his kit together, and was rushing to the door, when the phone rang. He was in two minds whether to answer it, but the second mind won, so he did. The caller was Tim Beasley.

"Hello David," he said.

"Arrgh, it's 'im!" replied David.

"What?" asked Tim.

"Arrgh, it's 'im!" repeated David. "It's what they used to say in the Dandy – or was it the Beano? – when Jonah came on-board ship."

"Oh."

"Don't mind me, Tim, I'm going mad. What's the matter?"

Tim's voice became hushed and secretive.

"I'm in a phone box. We're on a college trip to Birmingham to look around the galleries, and I've just had a flashback."

"Oh yeah?"

"Yeah! I just wandered off to look in this really swanky little private gallery, and there was this bloke in there tryin' to flog this painting to the owner, who was a real fruiter, but that's nuffin' to do wiv anyfin'."

"Go on."

"So this fruiter examines this picture and tells this little bloke who's trying to flog it that it's a forgery and worf nuffin', and the little bloke gets in a huff and tells him he's talking out of his arse. The fruiter starts wavin' his arms about and tells him to leave, so he goes stormin' out and slams the door."

"And?"

"Well, the fruiter comes over to me then, and starts going on about how he's been in the trade for years and knows a fake Picasso when he sees one."

"A Picasso?"

"Yep! But that's not why I phoned you. Listen. This little fat chap; I've seen him before. Remember when I told you and the police that the bloke who wanted the penis removed was tall and sporty with a moustache? Well, I just had this quick sort of memory flash, and he wasn't tall at all. It was this fat bloke that wanted the penis removed."

"A case of life imitating art if I ever heard one."

"Yer what?"

"Nothing, Tim. So where is this fat bloke now? You lost him in the crowds, I expect."

"No, I trailed him. He met up wiv this sort-of female thing - looked like a Russian shot-putter, and they caught the bus out of town. Well, we were about to go home anyway, so I caught the same bus, because it goes past my place, and they got off wiv this picture and guess what?"

"What?"

"They went into Meadow Fields Holiday Park. It's a caravan

173

site."

David beamed from ear to ear.

"Tim, you are wasted as a secret agent. You should be an artist. Did I say that right? Anyway, well done! I feel I should reward you in some way for this. You don't know what this means to me. Can I offer to buy another painting off you? Would that help?"

Tim was ecstatic. "Well, I'm a bit of a perfectionist, David, and they take me a fair time to do, so I don't have many on offer."

"How many *have* you got?"

"Erm, two, and you've already got one of 'em."

"So what's the other one?"

"It's a portrait of Jimmy Tarbuck."

"Gap-toothed Scouser?"

"Yep!"

"But why?"

"I did it as a commission, but the chap changed his mind when he saw it. It was his prognosis, I suppose."

"Prerogative. Never mind. I'll buy it. The usual fifty okay?"

"Wonderful!"

"It's a deal then. I'll pick it up tomorrow before the match. Better still, why don't you bring it? It'll be a nice day if the weather holds out. It's the last match of the season and I'm playing at number ten. The bar's open all day and there's a barbecue afterwards. Do you like cricket, Tim?"

"Yes."

"Never mind. It'll still be a good day though. Enville Hall. Half-ten. See you there."

David threw his cricket bag down and dialed Stourbridge Police Station. He needed to act quickly, before the Bearded Lady and Lee Marvin emptied their chemical toilet, hauled the calor gas bottle aboard and moved on.

Chapter 18

Ashes to Ashes

It was a perfect English late-summer's day. The sky was an undiluted cobalt blue, randomly scattered with pink-tinged, fluffy white clouds. Overhead, two hot-air balloons floated slowly across the landscape, snorting flame every now and again, like benign dragons. Above them, a small Cessna droned its way back to Twopenny Green aerodrome, its pilot no doubt waxing lyrical about the equally splendid view below.

Enville Hall and its cricket pitch glowed with a light that wouldn't have been out of place in Tuscany, and it was still only ten-thirty a.m. Young men in cricket whites were limbering up, strapping on their pads and practising their catches. The Mercedes rolled up behind the clubhouse, and David extricated his huge kitbag from the boot. Had the resident fly on the wall been stationed at the pavilion, it would have observed him pausing to pick up and pocket a small package, before walking around the front of the pavilion to meet Laz.

Laz was lounging in a whicker chair, looking smug. There was no trademark cigarette, and he was sipping an iced water, just to reinforce the illusion that he was endeavouring to live a clean life.

"Good morning, comrade!" he beamed. "I have here a sworn affidavit that no fag has touched my lips now for three weeks. If you can find anyone to testify against me, bring them on, and

176

make it snappy, good fellow. Now, correct me if I'm wrong, but what's your highest score this season? Do tell, prithee!"

"Bollocks!" replied David, collapsing into the adjacent seat. "It isn't over till the fat hypnotist sings."

Barry Suggs was next to join the party.

"Ah, if it isn't Don Bradman! Now listen. They're not a bad side, but the bowling's weak. They're also a bowler down, and under the Geneva Convention, we're allowing them to borrow one of our lads, so we've donated Spud. He's pretty good, as you know, but don't panic. You've learnt a lot since the first day, when he bowled a googly into your goolies."

David went as white as his clothing at the memory.

"Shit! My nemesis."

"Nonsense!" smiled Barry. "He's one of us. I can't see him being hard on you – his own team mate. If I were you, I'd go and buy him a drink, sharpish."

David had an open face, and Laz could always tell when a thought had flashed across it. He watched his friend rise from his seat and wander over towards the changing rooms, whistling nonchalantly as he did so. He emerged minutes later looking marginally more cheerful, just in time to see Tim Beasley arriving with a wrapped painting under his arm.

"Tell me that's a Picasso," implored David.

"'Fraid not, David," said Tim. "It's Jimmy Tarbuck."

"Oh well. Make yourself at home, Tim. Help yourself to a cup of tea. If you pop to the kitchen and ask nicely, Pauline will pour you one. I'll settle up with you in a bit. Just leave Tarbuck in the clubhouse on the far table and I'll collect it later. Now, if you'll excuse me, I've got to play cricket."

David strolled past Laz and Barry to find his team mates, so that he could watch the toss taking place. Laz wished him well and took a stroll himself, in the direction of the men's changing rooms.

Enville won the toss and elected to field. After a morning of hard graft in baking heat, they had succeeded in removing only four of the Ridgwood batsmen.

Meanwhile, Pauline lay prostrate in the kitchen, oblivious to it all, with an impressive collection of sandwiches strewn around her limp body. Her present condition was being observed and monitored by two independent witnesses. The ubiquitous fly on the wall, which had moved into the kitchen to investigate the various foodstuffs on offer, and Tim Beasley, who was the cause of Pauline's sorry state.

There are a handful of English expressions that can be called upon to describe clumsiness. A bull at a gate is one of them, as is a bull in a china shop. This random sample of two does rather indicate that bulls, as a class, have a tendency to rush into things without first considering the options, and the same could be said of Beasleys. Having caught three buses in order to reach the Enville ground, Tim was extremely dehydrated. David's offer of tea had therefore spoken to his depths. Whilst Ridgwood set about building their innings, he helped himself on a regular basis without so much as a 'by your leave', but it was when he visited the kitchen for the fourth time that morning that complications arose. Without once considering that there might be a person or persons lurking behind the kitchen door, he had barged in with such gusto that Pauline had no chance of taking avoiding action. The huge metal tray was the first victim. It immediately folded, ramming around three hundred and twenty-six sandwiches into Pauline's ample bosom. Not content with this, it then continued its arc and smashed her in the nose, sending her spectacles flying across the tiled floor. This, in turn, sent Pauline tumbling backwards over the pedal bin, causing the back of her head to connect with the larder unit. After that, she cared little about the slings and arrows of outrageous fortune, and resolved to take an impromptu nap.

Luckily, however, chaos and turmoil were no strangers to Tim Beasley, and he reacted the way he had always done in times of stress. He poured himself a cup of tea from the urn, and stood awhile in deep thought. The fly, meanwhile, untroubled by a social conscience, availed itself of the facilities.

* * *

At the end of the Ridgwood innings, the two teams returned to the pavilion for lunch, only to find that none was available. Barry Suggs, worried that the visiting side would think them inhospitable, dashed into the kitchen with a turn of speed that would have put Tim Beasley to shame, and was met by a scene of carnage. His leather-bottomed brogue shoes connected with several of the cucumber sandwiches, causing him to slide like a speed skater in the direction of the kitchen sink, until he was no longer able to keep upright. Not only did he fail to impress the Swedish judges, but he also fell heavily, right on top of Pauline, who was just in the process of waking from her dreamless sleep, only to be pole-axed for the second time. Tim Beasley, meanwhile, had missed most of the excitement, due to the fact that Barry had swung the door open with gusto, just as Tim had done previously, but this time the recipient had been Tim himself. Now the tally of seriously incapacitated kitchen visitors was an impressive three. The club secretary, Herbert Binns, arrived seconds later to witness the devastation, but ever the practical man, he invited both teams to salvage what they could from the floor whilst he called over the St. John's Ambulance volunteers.

Not having the stomach for food, David elected to sit outside and meditate. Laz, who was trying to instill confidence in his friend (but not too much, as there was a wager at stake) leant over to have a conspiratorial word about the techniques employed by the nearby Ridgwood spin bowler, when David suddenly recoiled in horror.

"You've just had a fag!"

"I swear I haven't touched one in three weeks, you cheeky bugger!"

"You've just had a bloody fag. I can smell it. I have a good nose. Turn out your pockets."

Laz indignantly did as he was told. The evidence failed to materialize.

"You forgot that little pocket on the side of your combat trousers," said David, suspiciously.

Barry Suggs staggered over to them, holding his back as if in pain, much to Laz's relief. He needed a change of subject urgently.

"What's up lads?" asked the injured first team captain.

"This snake in the grass has had a fag," snarled David. "Check that pocket, Barry."

Barry opened Laz's pocket and pulled out a packet of Benson and Hedges King Sized.

"They're not mine," protested Laz.

"Whose are they then?" asked David, "I can't wait to hear this one!"

"I found them in Spud's kitbag, in the men's changing rooms."

"Oh yeah? And what were you doing rummaging around in the men's changing rooms, you pervert?"

"Well," sighed Laz, "If you really want to know, I went in there to find Spud, because I suspected you'd gone in there to bribe him so that he'd bowl gently at you and allow you to knock your fifty runs, thus cheating me out of seeing you do your forfeit."

Now it was David that looked sheepish. "Well, that's preposterous!" he whined. "As if I'd resort to that kind of behaviour. So why did you steal Spud's fags then? Answer me that!"

"I was being public spirited, actually," insisted Laz. "Spud wasn't around, but I saw his kitbag – it's got SPUD written on it in six inch letters – and poking out of the top of it was this packet of fags. Well, I don't think it's right for a young lad like that to be smoking, especially as he's an Enville player, so I confiscated them for his own good."

Spud's mother, Edith, had been sitting nearby, and on hearing this, she stormed over to the table.

"My little Edward doesn't smoke!" she bellowed, her collection of chins wobbling furiously.

"Erm, he does, actually," replied David. He's always got one on the go down by the nets, not that I'd wish to get him into trouble or anything."

Edith was apoplectic now. "He does, does he? Wait till I get my hands on him. I'd like to know where he got them from as well. I packed his kit this morning, and they weren't there then, and I know he's got no money on him, because I always bring it. It tends to fall out of his whites, you see."

Spud, blissfully unaware of what was going on, walked straight into the eye of the storm.

"Hello, mom," he said cheerfully, "Can I have some money to get a coke from the bar before I start fielding?"

"Don't you coke me," she seethed. "What are these?" She produced exhibit A. Spud went white and began to stammer.

"Er, er, they're not mine, mom. David gave them to me just now, and asked me to go easy on him in the match so he could score fifty."

"Ha!" said Laz triumphantly. He meant it to sting.

"I don't smoke, but I kept them anyway, so as I could flog 'em to Daryl Jenkins after the game."

It was David's turn to look shaky now.

"You lying little bugger," he protested. "You said if I'd buy you some fags you'd consider it. I said I didn't need to because I'd actually found some by Laz's Porsche in the car park, and you could have those."

"They were *my* bloody fags!" shouted Laz. "They must have dropped out of my car when I got out."

The table went quiet, and all eyes were on Laz. He looked as guilty as a dog found rummaging in an upturned pedal bin.

"Oops!" he whispered, under his breath.

"Well that's bloody ironic," said David, who was reclaiming the moral high-ground for the umpteenth time in ten minutes. "Laz, the cheating bastard, drops his fag packet on the car park – the fags he assures us he no longer smokes – and then the shitbag steals his own packet from Spud's kitbag, and then smokes one of them. Look, there's one missing, and I can smell it on his breath."

Barry took a sniff and confirmed David's story, much to Laz's disgust.

"Oh, and who was it who bribed an under-aged boy with them then, Mr Perfect?" demanded Laz, dragging David unceremoniously from his high horse. "That's illegal, that is. You should be ashamed of yourself, especially as you claim to detest the filthy habit."

David was squirming now.

"Okay, okay! Neither of us comes out of this smelling good. I'll agree on that."

"No you don't," agreed Barry. "But there's no time to continue

182

this now. You're due on the pitch, Spud, and if I were you, David, I'd get myself down to the nets and do a bit of batting practice before Spud gets hold of you."

Spud just gave David a look that was intended to kill, or at least seriously maim. Edith was far less subtle, whacking her errant son around the head as he left to join his team mates, all of which meant that Enville's tail-ender batsman was not due for a smooth ride.

Whilst this drama had been unfolding on the terrace, another was unfolding within. The fit and muscular Barry had escaped the kitchen incident with only minor bruising to his back, but the equally unfortunate Tim and Pauline had not escaped so lightly. Pauline, one will recall, had lost consciousness for the first time in her life when she was felled by a large tub of ice cream. On the second occasion, it was a large tray of sandwiches. Not wishing to be type-cast as a food specialist, she elected to be anaesthetized the third time by a fifteen stone cricketer, and it was this same fifteen stone cricketer who had been responsible for Tim's temporary demise.

The kitchen was now a hive of activity, as the St.John's Ambulance staff tended to the fallen. First to come round was Tim, who had broken his glasses and had a bloodied nose. He was sat on an old chair with his head between his legs, repeating the words "Oh God!" like a mantra. Meanwhile, a young lady in a black uniform administered smelling salts to Pauline, which caused her to leap from the ground like a rocketing pheasant and shout, "Bugger off!" Eventually, she was persuaded to lie on a stretcher and be ferried outside to the first aid tent, where more specialist medicines were available. As she passed the terrace, numerous spectators enquired as to her health, and if she would be okay by teatime, when the tea and biscuits were due.

Overcome with feelings of remorse and guilt, Barry, still rubbing his back, made his way over to the tent to visit her in order that he could apologize.

"Are you okay, Pauline?" he asked. "It was totally my fault, charging in like that."

"My name is not Pauline," she assured him. "My name is Nogbad Olafson. You must help me up, sir. I must get back to my sheep."

"Ah, right!" frowned Barry, glancing over at the concerned young St.John's girl. This was worse than he had feared - he might have to prepare the tea and biscuits himself. He headed back to the pavilion to warn Herbert Binns, the club secretary, but instead found David, who was wearing a groove in the terrace decking by pacing to and fro. As first team captain, Barry instinctively knew when a pep talk was necessary.

"Ridgwood have knocked a big score for a one-day game," Barry informed David glumly. "We'll probably have to bat to the last man to stand a chance, and you'll all have to do your best for King and country. Luckily, our openers, 'Windy' Miller and Tranter, usually notch up a good ton between them, so that's a start."

Unfortunately, 'Windy' Miller and Tranter must have misheard and only managed to notch up a good ten, before they were sent inside for an early bath. Spratto and Brendon didn't do much better either, and had it not been for Rhys and Jamie, the side would have collapsed. The way it was going, David would have to knock fifty to save the game, let alone save his own skin. He sat, chewing his nails on a whicker chair next to the brooding and silent Laz, until he heard the inevitable 'Howzat?' There was only one batsman to go now before him, and David's stomach was doing somersaults. Donning his helmet, he stared, panic-stricken into Laz's eyes and begged to be wished good luck. The number nine batsman ambled out to the crease, and ambled back again four minutes later, dismissed by a fiery delivery from Spud, who seemed particularly driven. Ordinarily, his proud mother would applaud his every move, but today she just stared, stony-faced at her teacup.

David stood and theatrically crossed himself, the way Italian footballers always do when they're called on as a substitute. Then, swinging his bat around like a windmill blade to loosen up his shaking arm, he strode purposefully to the wicket, like a brave man walking to the gallows.

Thankfully, Spud's over was over, so to speak, and a weedy Ridgwood youth began his stint from the Enville Hall end. David wiped the sweat from his brow and took position, his legs trembling uncontrollably. The ball left the bowler's hand and bounced invitingly, but David tapped it down with a neat defensive stroke. Back in the pavilion, Barry shouted encouragement.

"Played, Dave. Bed yourself in, but don't take too long. We need the runs, and quick!"

The second delivery was a carbon copy of the first. There was no danger of it being on the wickets, so David lashed at it, and to his immense satisfaction, it went for four. Miffed now, the Weed chucked another ball that was frankly woeful, and David, his confidence on a high, thwacked it high in the air towards the boundary rope. A lone fielder scurried backwards in an attempt to catch it, but he tripped and fell, allowing the ball to sail home for a six. David snicked the next ball for a cheeky single, which meant that he was no longer facing the bowler. So far so good. The Ridgwood bowlers didn't appear to be up to much, as Barry had suggested. He just needed to keep a clear head and concentrate. The next over saw him score another four and two singles, and the one after that a six and three more singles. It was then that Ridgwood decided to retire the Weed in favour of Mister Blobby, a sixteen stone mound of blubber with a comb-over hairdo. He seemed to fancy himself as a spin specialist, and was taking the customary three step casual run-up to the wicket. David, by now oozing with confidence, put this down to the man's awful fitness levels, rather than an attempt to emulate Shane Warne. His first delivery confirmed David's suspicions. It was bowled with a spinner's style and with a spinner's pace, but thankfully, the one thing the ball didn't do was actually spin. It arrived at the crease with a note attached to it saying, 'Here I am for the taking. Please whack me out of the ground' so David did, causing a huge cheer to rise up from the pavilion. All of a sudden, Enville were in with a slim chance of winning this game, but the tail-enders would have to keep the impressive run rate going before the allocated overs ran out. David's partner, Ollie, calmed everyone's nerves with a couple of beautifully struck fours, and Mr Blobby was put out to grass by a disgruntled Ridgwood skipper, who seemed to be running out of ideas. After having a go himself, and being punished severely by both batsmen, he began to scratch his head, and, in desperation, called for Spud to do a bit more. Initially, he had been loath to employ this child for two reasons. Firstly, he was an on-loan Enville player, which meant that his heart wouldn't be in it, and secondly, he was no more than a kid, and an overweight one at that. Given the facts, he couldn't see him turning in a sterling performance, somehow. That said, he realized that beggars couldn't be choosers, and, as all else was failing, there was little alternative. After seeing him dismiss a couple of the middle order in determined fashion, he realized the error of his ways, and tossed the ball once more to Spud, who eyed up David like a peckish lion would eye up his lunchtime antelope, as he slowly paced out his run-up.

David swallowed audibly and glanced at the scoreboard. He still didn't fully understand what it all meant, if he was honest, but one thing was very apparent. Batsman number ten, a fellow by the name of Day, was on forty-nine runs. He began to breathe heavily, his head pounding with the heat inside his helmet, his screwed-up eyes watching every movement of Spud's body.

Spud turned, and began trundling up towards the quaking

batsman. What started as a slow trot soon became a mighty thundering run. By the time he arrived at the line, he must have been doing fifty miles per hour. Dust clouds gathered behind his sturdy frame, and then he took off, leaving the parched ground like a jumbo jet. There was a flash as his arm turned, followed by the clatter of ball upon wicket. David glanced behind him. The stumps were in disarray, and the bails had leapt a good yard backwards and were resting at jaunty angles in the grass. David just stood there, his mouth forming the perfect 'O' shape, just like Mike Gatting's had done when Warne got him out with the ball of the century. An overpowering feeling of déjà vu engulfed his deflated frame, and it was a good minute before his legs knew which way the pavilion was. Removing his helmet, David staggered back to rapturous applause, passing the last batsman en-route. An Enville victory seemed certain, thanks to his efforts, but sadly, he had lost his bet with Laz, or to be more accurate, he hadn't won it.

He pulled himself up the pavilion steps and removed his gloves whilst acknowledging Suzanne and Lauren, who were waving proudly from the bar. Neither understood what he'd achieved, but everyone else appeared to think it was worth applauding, so they joined in too. All around him, spectators were reaching over to slap his back or shake his hand, and none were more enthusiastic than Donald and Reg, who had just arrived in time to see David's heroic innings draw to a close.

"Well done," said Donald, handing him a parcel wrapped in brown paper. "I thought you'd like this. We won't go into detail for security reasons, but let's just say we found it in a caravan."

"Oh goodness!" sighed David, "Now that's a weight off my mind. Thank you *so* much!"

"Don't thank us, thank Tim Beasley, secret agent," laughed Reg. "And talking of whom, what's he done to himself? He looks as if he's done three rounds with Tyson."

"Lord knows!" replied David, shaking his head in disbelief.

"The chap is notoriously accident prone, apparently. And talk of the devil, here he comes now!"

Tim staggered over to greet David and the policemen, holding a hankie to his battered snout. His spectacles had been crudely repaired with masking tape.

"Well done, David," he said feebly. "I managed to watch some of your innin's, but I've been drifting in and out of consciousness. I feel really weak now. Mind you, it could be hunger. I haven't eaten all day."

"Never mind," said David, "There's a barbecue about to start, when Pauline gets it lit. I'll buy you a dozen hotdogs."

"She won't be lighting any barbies, David," said Tim sadly. "She finks she's a Viking sheep farmer called Nogbad at the moment. Her son, Ryan, is worried about her, but he reckons it's an improvement. When she was walloped by the ice cream tub, he says she fort she was a Victorian prostitute called Meg."

"Oh," said David. "Well, perhaps we can man the barbecue instead. Donald and Reg will be starving soon as well. They always are."

Barry Suggs came over to add his congratulations, just as a ripple of applause announced that the Enville tail-enders had secured victory.

"Well, young man, you've come a long way since our first nets practice. Well done! Sorry about your fifty though – you were so close, and this means you and Laz both have to do the forfeit."

"No," corrected David, "it means neither of us do, surely."

"Ordinarily yes, but you have both been found guilty of cheating, and as captain of this club, I declare that you must both agree to do whatever these here envelopes say. Agreed?"

"No."

"No from me as well."

"Very well, lads. You're no longer members of this cricket club."

"You can't do that," protested David and Laz in two part harmony.

"Can so. Are you doing the forfeits?"

"Open the envelopes," groaned David. "And after I got you out of the shit with the cops, Barry, really!"

Barry opened the envelopes slowly and with great relish, like a presenter at the Oscars.

"Larry. You must run round the perimeter rope stark naked."

"What? You must have the wrong envelope. I'm not doing that!"

"You heard. Right, David. Well I never! *You* must run round the pitch naked. Great minds think alike eh?"

David was mortified. Obviously, it would have been great fun forcing Laz to do it, but it wasn't something he would contemplate doing himself. He was beginning to get angry with his friend for asking him to do it; Laz knew full well that he was shy about his appendage. David liked to keep it in his Y Fronts unless he was peeing. He was happy for Suzanne to inspect it, of course, in the sanctity of their boudoir, but he wasn't so keen on the filthy unwashed public sizing it up. There was another issue at stake too – and it was altogether more sensitive. Laz was the proud owner of a rather large specimen, so parading it around the pitch for all and sundry to gawp at would probably appeal to him in a strange way. David had often glanced down at his friend's equipment as they stood at the urinals together in restaurants, though he had cleverly prevented Laz from reciprocating by holding his own as a squaddie would surreptitiously hold a cigarette whilst on guard duty – knuckles upwards, so as to hide the thing. What had always stuck in his mind was how big and black Laz's member was, for a white man. David had even suspected at one stage that, somewhere along the line, Laz had been given a penis transplant from an African donor. Either that or he had accidentally left it dangling out of his shorts while he sunbathed. The thing just didn't seem natural, and it had crossed David's mind that Laz could even have been the leader of the dreaded Black Penis Gang, had such an organization existed. The problem now facing David was exacerbated by the fact that his own equipment was meagre by comparison. Indeed, on cold days it resembled a sparrow's nest with an acorn in it.

David wasn't the only one present to be experiencing a severe attack of nerves, however. Laz did possess a todger that he would gladly show to all and sundry – so proud was he of it – but something else was exercising him to the point of sheer panic. Whilst his friend was tall, thinnish and fairly fit after a season of cricket, he was overweight and completely unfit after many seasons of heavy smoking and drinking. In a nutshell, what he was exercised about was the exercise. He feared it might be the end of him. The perimeter rope of a full-sized cricket pitch is deceptively lengthy. From the pavilion bar it may look nothing, but to run around it naked was another kettle of fish altogether.

"Can't we call it a draw and forget about it?" he asked, his voice all of a tremble.

"No," said Barry, trying to keep a straight face, which was difficult, as he had been born with a crooked one. "Rules is rules. You asked me to keep these envelopes and preside over this bet, and that's what I'm doing. Get 'em orf."

"Erm, I've got to see Donald and Reg," interrupted David. "They have a special package for me and it's very important."

"We'll pop it in the pavilion and ask the steward to keep an eye on it," said Donald, eager to help as always. "Don't worry."

"Erm, I need to see Tim as well, he's got an important package for me too, haven't you Tim?" David appeared to have something in his eye, which Tim duly ignored.

"It's okay, Dave," replied Tim, "I'll put it wiv the officer's package till you get back. Meanwhile, shall I light the barbecue, being as Pauline's incapacitated? If I don't eat soon, I'm gonna faint."

"No you bloody well can't!" David insisted. "I don't trust you - Donald, *you* can light the thing. It takes half an hour before the coals are ready, so you'd better get on with it, and I suppose we ought to get this over with whilst there aren't too many folks on the terrace, ogling us. Tim, if you're really that desperate, go and make a bit of toast to keep you going, and check there's no one behind the bloody door when you enter the kitchen, there's a good chap."

Inhaling profoundly, David began to remove his cricket whites, while Laz sat down on the grass to remove his trainers, so that he could get his trousers off. It was taking all of Barry's resolve not to double up with laughter, while Reg just bit his lip and looked away.

"The one good thing about this," said David, desperate to find a silver lining, "is that, for the first half, we are heading *away* from the pavilion, so they'll just see our arses."

He quickly removed the Y Fronts and covered his privates with his cupped hands, in stark contrast to Laz, who removed his boxers with minimal fuss and just stood there letting it all hang out. Reg turned around again just in time to be given an eyeful, and gasped, "Jeez! I wondered where my truncheon had got to," before striding off to help Donald with the barbecue.

David and Laz turned and began to trot away from the pavilion, acting as nonchalantly as they could. It was almost teatime, and the golden light that was bathing the pitch made the brickwork of Enville Hall glow. The sun was huge and low in the sky, and the hot air balloons had sailed off into the distance, heading for home.

Birds trilled, the horses in the nearby fields whinnied contentedly, and, elsewhere at least, all was right with the world.

"You know, this is quite liberating really, when you get used to it," laughed David. "There's a lovely breeze."

"Can you do the talking?" asked Laz, who was lagging behind. "I can run, breathe and talk, but not all at the same time."

"This is my favourite time of day, you know," David continued. "This sunset is very Mediterranean, don't you think, and I love that orangey-pink colour that old bricks go at this time of the evening. I'd love to do a painting of the old hall, when I get time, and capture that hour when the world goes all golden. That's when England is at its very best, and minutes later, it's all disappeared, and everything goes flat and grey. When you think about it, the Impressionists really had to paint at speed to capture a scene such as this, before the light changed. It makes you appreciate their skill, doesn't it?

"Dave," said Laz, gasping for air now.

"Yeah?"

"We' are currently running around a cricket pitch, stark-bollock-naked. I don't need a lecture from Brian Sewell at the same time."

"Sorry, I was just trying to take my mind off it."

David slowed the pace in order that his flagging friend could run alongside him. Laz glanced down at David's wiggling privates and smiled a secretive smile.

"You mustn't keep running yourself down, you know," he panted. "The only reason yours looks tiny is because it's next to mine. Given fairer competition, you could hold your own, so to speak. A pre-pubescent child, for example, would be chuffed to have one that big, I bet."

"Gee thanks."

192

"Don't mention it. It's probably just shrunken due to the cold. I daresay it's the average size, once excited. How big does it get?"

David winced. "I suppose I can manage nearly six on a good day."

"There you are then!" replied Laz. "Six is very apt for a cricketer. More or less average, I would have said."

"I was talking metric," sighed David.

"Oh!"

The two runners ran in silence for the next minute or so, Laz wearing a quite hideous smirk and David deep in thought. They had reached the sight screens at the far end of the pitch, which meant they were on the home straight. David instinctively cupped his hands around his member again, which seriously impeded his once-fluent jogging style. The pavilion was still just a small block of white in the distance, but Laz could already tell that there was a very large contingent of players and guests gathered outside and making a lot of noise. Then, his facial expression changed from a mixture of exhaustion and sheer embarrassment to one of concern.

"Something is going on!" he gasped. "They're not looking at us. They've got their backs to us."

Upon hearing this, David began to experience mixed emotions. Part of him, namely the private part, was relieved that he wasn't the centre of attention, but another part of him was secretly disappointed.

"Bloody hell!" he exclaimed, "Look! See that plume of thick black smoke coming out of the roof?"

"Oh shit, you're right."

"The pavilion is on fire!"

"And it's all my fault," groaned David.

"How can it be your fault? You're running around the pitch

naked."

"I told Tim Beasley to make toast."

"Eh? So what?"

"You don't know Tim Beasley. He's like Jonah from the Beano, - or was it the Dandy? The sailors used to say, "Aargh! It's him!" when he came on board, because within five minutes, he'd accidentally sink their ship."

"I remember him! It was the Dandy, I think. Look, can you see? Donald and Reg are trying to keep everyone calm."

"All the raffle prizes will be incinerated," said David. "I was donating two Tim Beasley originals, but I haven't broken it to him yet."

Laz grinned at his naked friend. "I've seen one of them. My bottle of Blue Nun won't be the last raffle item to be claimed then. I'm spared that embarrassment."

The two exhausted naturists were within spitting distance of the finishing post now, but hardly anyone seemed interested. They were far more concerned about the pavilion, their kitbags, the changing rooms full of clothing and possessions, the buffet, the raffle prizes and the thousands of pounds worth of equipment within.

"Oh Christ!" yelled David, his hands deserting his organ in order to cover his open mouth. "The Picasso!"

They had finally reached their destination, and were able to stagger over to their discarded clothes and quickly dress, unheeded by the anxious throng. As they did so, Donald, his face blackened with smoke, dashed heroically from the building carrying a brown paper package in one hand and dragging a distraught Tim Beasley with the other. Tim, whose spectacles were now blacker than Suzanne's Ray Bans, was still clutching what looked like a barbecue briquette, but had once been a slice of Sunblest. Donald handed him to a waiting St.John's Ambulance lady, before picking his way through the crowd to find David.

"I saved your picture," he smiled, wiping a filthy hand across his sweating brow. I couldn't save Gary Glitter, I'm sorry to say."

David thanked Donald brokenly and flung his arms around him. "It was probably for the best," he smiled.

"You're not kidding," said Donald. "I don't know much about art, but in my opinion, it was shite. One eye up here, the other down there."

"Bloody hell!" panicked David, grasping the policeman's blackened lapels with both hands, "That sounds like the Picasso. You do know which is which don't you?"

"Relax, I know which is which," Donald assured him, "and personally, I preferred the Tim Beasley, just about, but what do I know?"

David calmed down a little. "Well, it was funnier, I suppose. How's the pavilion?"

Donald shook his head sadly. "It's ruined. The fire brigade hasn't even arrived yet, and it's already beyond repair. Wooden structure you see. It was a fire trap."

"It's going to cost a fortune to put all this right, Donald."

"Yep! It's made four Enville cricket teams homeless, and the footballers use it in the winter too. It's a tragedy for the community, that's a fact!"

"Are they well insured?"

"Don't think so."

David stood, deep in thought.

"That package of yours would buy a pavilion and a ton of equipment, I bet."

"And the rest!" replied Donald.

"Perhaps it was never discovered at that caravan after all," suggested Laz mischievously.

Donald scratched his blackened pate. "Steady on, son. That's impossible. I've already reported that it was found."

"Then maybe the fire just destroyed it."

"Laz, mate, they send the forensic boys in with magnifying glasses after a fire like this. You can't fool them!"

Laz glanced around him conspiratorially. Apart from Reg, there were no eavesdroppers.

"Okay," he whispered. "Here's the plan. I know this really dodgy German art dealer. Dave, do you reckon you could get this copied by next Friday?

THE END.

Books in the David Day Series.

A NASTY BUMP ON THE HEAD

Eleven-year-old David Day finds the curmudgeonly toy shop owner, Miss Kettle, murdered in her shop. He duly informs Scotland Yard, only to bump into her in Tenbury Wells the following week.

MONET TROUBLE

First year art student David Day is persuaded to forge a Monet painting by the mysterious Lord Hickman, but unknown to either of them, several other artists have the same idea.

VINCENT GOUGH'S VAN

An art college murder mystery of Shakespearian proportions, littered with psychic sewing teachers, entrail-painting students and lesbian assassins.

THE CURSE OF TUTTON COMMON

David sets about trying to improve Britain's worst museum, and ably assisted by a cat named Hitlerina, he discovers an ancient Egyptian tomb in South Staffordshire.

PAINTING BY NUMBERS

Thirty-year-old David is having a mid-life crisis, made worse by the fact that his art studio has exploded, and the ninety-year-old 'paint by numbers' enthusiast he has befriended is not what he seems.

STEALING THE ASHES

Forty–year-old David Day overhears two Australian cricketers plotting to steal the Ashes, and, ably hampered by Laz, he tries his best to thwart their plans.

Written and soon to be published;

THE HUNT FOR GRANDDAD'S HEAD

The prequel to Nasty Bump! Daleks have invaded Brierley Bank, but David harnesses their power to see off the neighborhood bully.

...and two new novels featuring a new hero!

THE CURIOUS TALE OF THE MISSING HOOF

Writer Adam Eve hires a pantomime horse costume, but forfeits his deposit when he loses one of the hooves. His obsessive efforts to locate it create mayhem!

MR. MAORI GOES HOME

Adam Eve's hell-raising uncle has died and left him a substantial amount of money – on condition that he returns a rare Maori carving to New Zealand.

For more information, email gt@geofftristram.co.uk

Tarmac

P.O. Box 8, Millfields Road, Ettingshall, Wolverhampton WV4 6JP

Dear Readers,

Well, he's been and done it again. You have to admire the chap in a begrudging kind of way, I must admit. Every time he asks, I say to him, "No more sponsorship I'm afraid. We haven't had a single enquiry about building a new motorway off the back of these expensive ads in your books, presumably because only six or seven people ever buy them and none of them are cabinet ministers."

Then he gets all upset - you can actually see the tears welling up in his eyes, and he replies, "That's okay, Chris. You've been wonderful to me over the years, commissioning me to fake all those highly-illegal, signed impressionist masterpieces on the cheap for your secret villa in Tuscany, rather than see me starve. I'll just leave now, and I won't darken your door again, though I still think that Midnight Blue really suited it. And try not to think about those poor, wide-eyed little cricketing ragamuffins when I have to inform them that they won't get their new nets after all. Well, goodbye Mr Reynolds. Merry Tristmas from me and Tiny Tim, our little disabled wicket keeper!"

Well, call me an old softy, but I always end up calling him back and pressing a few quid into his grimy, paint-spattered hand, hoping against hope that he doesn't spend it on drink. (I've heard that he's that kind of artist.) I'm finished now though. Enough is enough. We've done our bit. He can tap up some other sucker next time. Stealing the Ashes? Stealing from Tarmac more-like. Bah, humbug!

Chris 'Ebeneezer' Reynolds
Company Accountant.

The David Day Fan Club

Those of you who have read a David Day book will know how addictive they can become. At first, you think you can take them or leave them – you are an adult with a modicum of willpower, after all, and no mere book is going to rule your life. Quite soon though, you realize that you've started reading a quick chapter while you're in the bath or the lavatory. From there it is but a short step to the torch under the bed sheets at midnight and the paperback hidden inside your desk at the office. You'll find yourself reading the final chapter extra slowly to make it last longer, savouring every word and even reading good bits twice. Then, when you can stall no further and the book is finished, you will go through an awful mourning process, whereupon an intense craving will kick in. You'll need more and you'll need it NOW. Bad-tempered due to the crippling withdrawal symptoms, you'll probably complain that the author isn't nearly prolific enough for your voracious appetite, and begin to call him rude names. Extreme cases have even been known to try and climb the walls in anguish. Friends will turn against you because you will insist on regurgitating the plots *ad nauseam* while they're trying to watch television. It will get so bad that you might seriously consider a spell in a rehab clinic, or maybe a course of hypnotism.

Well, help is at hand. Why not join the David Day Fan Club? It's a bit like Alcoholics Anonymous. You sit around in a circle and confess, "My name is Deirdre Sponge and I'm a David Day fanatic." (Obviously, you don't say this if your name is*n't* Deirdre Sponge. That was just an example.) Then the others get up and hug you, with a bit of luck.

If you email me at gt@geofftristram.co.uk I'll keep your name on file and let you know when a new book is due to be released into the wild. Unlike other authors who are now too important – people such as J.K. Rowling and William Shakespeare for example, I promise to be approachable, grateful, humble, and always write back. That's with the proviso that you tell me my books are great, of course. I don't want any sour-faced old scrooges writing in to tell me I'm rubbish and that I deserve to be horse-whipped on the steps of my club. Maybe I could cope if you've spotted a glaring error, or a bit you didn't think made perfect sense, but obviously, I'd prefer it if you to told me how a paragraph had made you wet yourself on the train, or prevented you from leaping off a high building to certain death. You can suggest things that David can get up to in future stories, if you wish. I might even write *you* into a book. After all, most of my characters are based on real people, believe it or not! Oops! Shouldn't have admitted that – now no one will believe that legal disclaimer in the small print at the beginning.

Anyway, I'll leave it with you. The offer's there. You can lead a horse to water but you can't make it drink, as my Granny Bertha often attempted to say. I hope you've enjoyed 'Stealing the Ashes'. It's 'The Hunt for Granddad's Head' next, which is the prequel to 'A Nasty Bump on the Head', and if *that* doesn't make you laugh, I'll refund your money.

That was a joke by the way. You have to be so careful in this litigious age. I need the money for a new conservatory - I can't afford to give it back. The bookshops keep forty percent anyway. And another thing - will you stop lending my books to everyone when you've finished them? Let them buy their own. I'm never going to be another J.K. Rowling at this rate.

Geoff Tristram.

We at Leemoore Scissor Lifts - rather predictably, it has to be said - install scissor lifts. That's why our company is called Leemoore Scissor Lifts – the clue is in the name.

If we had decided to call our company, for example, Leemoore Tropical Fish Limited, we doubt very much whether anyone would ever ring us to buy a scissor lift, and we'd soon be bankrupt, unless of course we quickly got hold of some tropical fish and sold those instead, just to make ends meet until the scissor lift punters realized that we had a whole warehouse full of the things crying out for a good home.

So there you are. It's a long shot, but if you *do* need one – a scissor lift that is, we're the folks you need to talk to.

There's a bit of space left, so we might as well fill it - we've paid enough for it after all. We got conned into coughing up for this advert because our son, Ryan, plays for Enville Cricket Club with Geoff Tristram's son, Jamie, only our Ryan's a far better batsman than Jamie, it has to be said. We know that we're biased, but it's a fact. Ask anyone.

Er, that's it.

LEEMOORE
SCISSOR LIFTS LTD

Unit 52B, Wellington Industrial Estate, Bean Road,
Coseley WV14 9EE
Telephone 01902 664444

* Free tropical fish with every order over £10,000

203

'**A** Nasty Bump on the Head' has already sold a few thousand copies, and 'Stealing the Ashes' looks set to do even better, so that means, conservatively speaking, a potential two thousand classic car restorations as a result of this advertisement. With this in mind, I am already actively recruiting staff and seeking palatial new premises.

Estimating that my proposed team of thirty restorers could easily handle all of the work that my ad would undoubtedly bring in, I decided to take up cricket again after twenty years of inactivity.

It has been a lifelong ambition to win some form of trophy, and to this end I decided to manufacture the Enville wicket covers at my workshop, free of charge, in the vain hope that the club might present me with the Best Bowler Award. In spite of my saving the club bucket-loads of money, for some inexplicable reason they saw fit to present the trophy to a chap who was good at bowling instead.

However, thanks to my indomitable spirit and superior welding skills, I have now created the prestigious Richard Spratley 'Butterfingers' Cup for the most woeful fielding display of the season, knowing full well that I am sure to win it.

That's sorted then. Now all I need to do is sit back and wait for all those lucrative car restoration orders to flood in!

R. J. SPRATLEY

Classic Car Restoration & Wheel Refurbishment

*Unit 2, The Hayes Business Park, Lye, West Midlands DY9 8NR

Telephone 01384 893576

Email rjspratley@hotmail.com

*But not for much longer, eh?

With grateful thanks to the following individuals and companies who have kindly donated money in order to help Enville C.C. buy much-needed equipment.

*****

T. Saxon & Co. – Chartered Accountants

43, Hagley Road, Stourbridge DY8 1QR

01384 373217

*****

Stourbridge Music Centre

(and Stourbridge Music School)

Telephone 01384 375656

*****

Blackwell Tree Solutions

Telephone 01384 893186

www.blackwelltreesolutions.com johnupatree@aol.com

*****

Arron Print

Telephone 01527 67295 www.arronprint.co.uk

*****

The Badger Bite

"The best little cross-country race of the year by far."

(And a Limited Edition Trist cartoon for every runner!)

www.badgerbite.co.uk

*****

206

"Er, this is Jamie Tristram. Can *I* have an advert in this book?"

"No."

"Can I have an X Box game then?"

"No."

"Shitbag."

"What did you just call me?"

"Nuffin'."